MW00815125

The Life & Times of Jim Henry Shore

a novel based on history

LAWRENCE DAVIS

LYSTRA BOOKS
& Literary Services

The Life and Times of Jim Henry Shore
Copyright © Lawrence Davis 2020
All rights reserved.

ISBN, paperback 978-1-7336816-5-0
ISBN, ebook 978-1-7336816-6-7

Library of Congress Control Number: 2020901874

This is a work of historical fiction, based on family stories as well as document-ed events. The author has added his imagination and experience of human nature to his research and memory.

All photos courtesy of the author's family, unless otherwise noted.

Other than brief excerpts for review, no material from this book may be re-produced in any medium without written permission from the author. Please send your permission requests to the publisher at the address shown below.

Book design by Kelly Prelipp Lojk

Publisher, Lystra Books & Literary Services, LLC
391 Lystra Estates Drive
Chapel Hill, NC 27517
lystrabooks@gmail.com

———— •◆• ————

*This book is dedicated to my father, **Egbert Lawrence Davis, Jr.**, and those who share his interest in family history. His interest was reflected as early as age twelve when he'd saddle up his pony and ride a day's journey alone to stay with his Yadkin County relatives in order to get to know them and farm life. He especially enjoyed visits with his grandfather James "Jim" Henry Shore because "he would talk to me."*

———— •◆• ————

CONTENTS

PROLOGUE VII

1 Salt .1

2 Fayetteville 5

3 Homeward 17

4 Yadkinville 24

5 Losses 28

6 Jim Henry's Dilemma 31

7 Saltville 34

8 Duty 38

9 Junior Recruit 46

10 Fall of Camp Vance 49

11 Captive 53

12 Hell 65

13 Release 87

14 Hard Times 100

15 Seeking Passage 109

16 Voyage to Panama 117

17 Panama 131

18 The Pacific 134

19 San Jose 138

20 Farming in California 143

21 Leaving California 150

22 The Return Home 155

AFTERWORD 167

BIBLIOGRAPHY 171

——— • ◆ • ———
THE LIFE & TIMES OF JAMES HENRY SHORE
——— • ◆ • ———

As told by his great-grandson
Lawrence Davis

AUTHOR'S NOTE: I have heard stories about my great-grandfather all of my life. If a person lives in this world as long as someone remembers him, then James Henry Shore may be eternal. For this account of his life, I draw on family stories, as well as the more official records of censuses, archives, and historical records. When I give voice to Jim Henry and imbue him with emotion and thoughts, it is because I feel I know him and he tells the tales of his life and his times through me. Besides, it is well known that a good story is worth improving upon.

$$PROLOGUE$$

Principal Albert Martin called off school at Boonville High School on Monday, March 2, 1936, so that those who wished to attend the funeral of Jim Henry Shore could do so.

The funeral attendees knew they were there to celebrate a life significant to their community, as important as Daniel Boone himself, from whom Boonville drew its name.

Members of the community called him "Mr. Shore," as he had outlived everyone who called him "Jim Henry." He was born on February 20, 1847, the first child of John Benjamin (known as Jack) Shore and Eunice Reece Shore. When Jim Henry was born, they lived in a log cabin Jack built three miles southeast of Boonville. James Knox Polk was president, Abraham Lincoln was a circuit lawyer in Illinois, and Robert E. Lee was superintendent at West Point, overseeing the education of young men from both North and South.

Jim Henry acquired his formal education in one-room schoolhouses between November and March over a span of less than ten years. While in school, he fell in love with his classmate, Julia Williams, born six days earlier than he on a neighboring farm. Circumstances beyond their control separated them for long periods of time. Yet their love and devotion to each other continued undiminished.

Some people wondered how he came to enlist in the Confederate army against the wishes of his family, why in his adulthood he

attended the Baptist church while his parents and siblings continued in the Quaker church, and why he was a Democrat when most
of his family members, like most Yadkin County residents, were
strongly Republican. The evidence suggests that it was his love for
Julia that led him to reject the advice of his family and members
of the Quaker community and to submit to the conscription law,
which required him at age eighteen to enlist in the Confederate
Army. The result was his capture by Union forces, a forced march
to Tennessee, a long ride in cattle cars to prison in Chicago's noto-
rious Camp Douglas.

This book will explain all those things, and more, about the
life and times of Jim Henry Shore.

Salt

Jim Henry worked all morning with his father, Jack Shore. It was winter, January 1863, and Jack said it wasn't too early to look ahead to the next growing season. There was always work to do on a farm. Besides that, Jack was planning a trip down to Fayetteville. He'd sell his whiskey along the way and bring back a wagonload of salt. He'd count on Jim Henry to keep the farm going in his absence, and to take care of his mother and the four younger boys. It made Jim Henry proud to be thought a man, but he wished he could go along on his father's travels. Jack's stories about the places he went and the things he saw gave Jim Henry a yen to see beyond the tree line of their farm and the town of Boonville.

"Let's head to the house," Jack said. "Your mama will have dinner ready."

They were halfway between the barn and the house when they heard hoofbeats and saw their neighbor, Jesse Dobbins, riding hard toward them. Jesse was a few years older than Jim Henry, from a good Quaker family. He was Jack's assistant in the salt business.

Jesse reigned his horse in and slid off. "Jack, I can't go to Fayetteville. The sheriff just served me with a conscription notice. They say I got to join the Confederate Army."

The war had been going on for nearly two years. Jim Henry had seen for himself how North Carolina's secession from the

Front view of the 1847 log cabin built by Jim Henry's father, Jack Shore, for his family. Located approximately four miles southeast of Booneville, North Carolina.

union had forced people to take sides. The Quaker faith he'd been brought up in was against war in any form and opposed to slavery. But other neighbors in the county were strong for the Confederacy. Jim Henry knew his mother and father didn't see the issues in exactly the same way. Mama was clear and plain-spoken under their roof. Dad didn't argue with her, but sometimes he said something to Jim Henry that let him know he'd seen enough of the world to know right and wrong weren't so simple.

When the governor appointed Jack Shore to be a salt commissioner, that position came with an exemption from service in the army, so his parents could exist in peace. Until now, Jesse had been exempted, too, because of his Quaker faith and his position as Jack's assistant, so the news that he'd been conscripted came as a shock.

"Maybe you ought to go with me anyway," Jack said. "Get out of the area for a while."

"It's not that simple. The militia everywhere will have the names of all the conscripts. I could be arrested on the road. I'll have to hide out. Besides, I need to be meeting with some other fellows to make plans to go north and cross the lines together. We are trying to get up a crowd and hope there will be safety in numbers. Young Jim Henry should consider doing the same thing before he reaches the conscription age next year."

"You really think things are that bad?" Jack put a hand on Jim Henry's shoulder.

"The militia has arrested and even killed deserters, and now they are after conscripts," Jesse said. "I don't plan to hang around and get killed. You know I won't fight for slavery or for secession. If I must fight, it will be for the Union."

"Well, I can't ask a man to risk his life to haul salt," Jack said. "You'd best get on with your business, and I'll figure a way to get on with mine. I will miss having you with me. As for Jim Henry, he is still just fifteen and doesn't have to have his life on the line for a little while yet."

"He's old enough to take my place in the salt business. He can drive my team and wagon. You are welcome to use them," Jesse said.

Jim Henry's heart jumped. It felt wrong to be happy that Jesse had to run away from home, but Jim Henry couldn't help himself. He gave his father an expectant grin.

Jack reflected for a moment and said, "Much obliged to you, Jesse. We'll take you up on it. Right, son?"

"Yes sir!" Jim Henry said.

"It's noon," Jack said. "Time for dinner. Please join us, Jesse."

"Sorry, but I have to set up a camp out in the woods right away. Word is out for other men to join me so we can head out soon. Can you get by my place to pick up the wagon and mules this afternoon?"

"We'll do it." Jack put an arm around Jesse. "You just take good care of yourself. Let's hope all this is over soon and you can come back home."

"I'll take good care of your mules and wagon," Jim Henry said.

"You better." Jesse grinned at Jim Henry, then remounted and rode off as fast as he'd come.

2
Fayetteville

On Saturday, January 31, 1863, exactly three weeks before his sixteenth birthday, Jim Henry perched himself on Jesse Dobbins's wagon, clucked to the mules, and fell in behind his father's wagon. He and Jack were beginning the longest trip either of them had ever undertaken to the largest town they had ever seen. If Jim Henry was a little frightened, he was more excited, but he didn't want his father to see either emotion. He needed to match his father's calm determination.

Each wagon carried three barrels of whiskey in its bed. Due to the low value of crops and lack of an efficient means of transporting bulk cargo, Jack used his distillery, or 'stillery, to convert corn to whiskey and apples to brandy, most of which he hauled east from the hills to markets in the flatlands. His best customer was Mr. N.A. Chapin, proprietor of the Salem Tavern, in neighboring Forsyth County. Jack also took whiskey to nearby Panther Creek, where he sold it to Nicholas Williams, who aged, mixed, and bottled it for sale under his brand name, Old Nick. To get a better price, Jack had occasionally hauled his whiskey 130 miles to Cheraw, South Carolina, where the river's name changed from the Yadkin to the Pee Dee, which was deep enough to support steamboat service to Georgetown on the coast.

Jack brought home stories of adventures he'd had along the way, of people he'd met and food he'd eaten, all of which sounded exotic to Jim Henry. Now he'd have some adventures of his own and see new sights for himself.

But first, he must say good-bye to his mother. She and his younger brothers stood in the yard to watch him and his dad leave. His mother, Eunice, made no secret of her pride in her oldest son. She had taught him to read and write at an early age, and she conveyed her deep Quaker faith to him.

Jim Henry had a speech ready to make. He held his hat in his hands, so they wouldn't shake. "Mama, I'll miss you while we're gone. Brothers, please help our mom out in running the farm until Dad and I return. Just be glad it's not yet planting season! We can't wait to see y'all when we return."

As Jim Henry's team of mules turned into the road that led away from home, he felt the barrels of whiskey shift. He'd have to get accustomed to the load. He and his father had piled hay under, over, and around the whiskey barrels to protect them, and to provide themselves with a bed for the night, when needed. The hay was also handy for feeding the mules in case the snow made natural forage inaccessible.

They spent Saturday night, with Jack's parents on their farm, ten miles to the east near Flint Hill. After an early family devotional service on Sunday, February 1, they mounted their wagons and headed toward Glenn's Ferry, which would take them across the Yadkin River.

—◆—

Once across the river, their route took them past the Wade Williams farm. The Williams family once lived near the Shores, but had moved when Mr. Williams, a slaveholder, fell out with his Quaker neighbors. He still owned the farm adjacent to the Shores', but the Williams family had moved to another home some ten miles away, too far for the families to see each other often. Jack had no grudge against Wade, though, and Jim Henry was glad when his dad said they'd take a rest stop and visit. Wade Williams was a former state representative and Jack would want to talk politics.

Jim Henry had a different reason for being glad to visit the Williams household. He and Wade's daughter, Julia, were both born in February 1847 on adjacent farms. They grew up together and started school together at a one-room schoolhouse. They shared a desk and became inseparable, until the time when the Williams family moved away.

When they were six years old, their teacher, Reverend Bond, asked Julia to give Jim Henry an oral arithmetic quiz. When it was over, she reported to the reverend, "Sometimes it takes him a while, but he always gets the right answer."

At age ten, Julia had given Jim Henry another assessment he would never forget. It came on an unusually warm March day in 1857, near the end of the fourth and final year they were together in school. The teacher took the students on a field trip, during which they walked through a beautiful garden. Jim Henry and Julia found themselves walking together and instinctively reaching out and holding hands. Julia looked at him, smiled, and with a musical lilt in her voice said, "I love you, Jim Henry." He was so moved with joy he could hardly recall what he said in response.

Soon after that, the Williams family moved away and Jim Henry began to attend a different school, the Bond School.

As Jack and Jim Henry pulled up to the house, Julia Williams came running out, her brown hair flowing behind her, blue eyes sparkling, and a huge smile on her face.

Mr. Williams followed his daughter and called a hello. Jack got down from his wagon and the men shook hands. Jim Henry slid off his seat. He felt his face go hot when Julia smiled at him.

"Julia, show Jim Henry where he can get water for the mules," Mr. Williams said.

Nothing in the world could have made Jim Henry happier than to have a few minutes alone with Julia.

"You going far?" she asked as he drew a bucket of water from a well behind the barn.

"We're going to Fayetteville," he said. "Buying salt. I'm Dad's helper now."

"That's so far away. Aren't you scared?"

"No. I always wanted to see the world beyond Boonville." He was boasting, and he knew his mother would scold him for puffery, but he couldn't seem to help himself.

"Your face is as red as your hair," Julia said. She'd always teased him about his hair, but he'd never minded when it was her.

He set down the second bucket of water he'd drawn and looked into her eyes. "I sure do miss you, Julia."

She reached for his hand and held it in both of hers. He knew she felt the same way. Before he could speak again, he heard a shrill whistle. "That's my dad. It means he wants me to hurry up."

Jim Henry carried a bucket of water in each hand and Julia carried one for him. The mules drank deeply, nodded, and shook their heads.

Julia looked at Jim Henry and said, "Won't you stay and go to church with us? A bit of Methodist preaching might be good for you."

It was Jack who answered her. "Church would do us good, but we need to get to the Salem Tavern before dark. We hope to be there in time to get a bed. It may be our last chance to sleep in one for a while."

He and Wade Williams exchanged a few more words, and Jim Henry took Julia's hand again. She leaned over and kissed him on the cheek. He and his dad were several miles down the road before Jim Henry knew it. He couldn't get over that kiss.

—◆—

In less than an hour, Jack slowed his wagon and called back to Jim Henry. "See that house? That's Tyre Glenn's plantation."

Jim Henry looked down a long lane and saw the biggest house he'd ever seen at the end of it. He knew about Tyre Glenn, a former slave trader and land broker from the Deep South, who settled along the Yadkin and built one of the largest plantations in western North Carolina. It included a quarry, a dam and grist mill, and a ferry across the Yadkin. After passing the mansion, Jack and Jim Henry descended for more than a mile into and across the beautifully cultivated bottomland to the Yadkin River. Although Tyre Glenn owned 360 slaves, there were none visible in the fields. It was Sunday.

Jim Henry's family included a former slave, a young man named Jim. Jim helped Jack with farm work and slept in the loft with the Shore boys. Jim Henry had seen slaves, dark-skinned people who moved like shadows and seemed to him to lead a mysterious existence. His mother's teaching was that they were just like him and his brothers, God's children. But he'd heard other people say differently, and he didn't know which side he'd take, if called upon to do so.

They left Yadkin County by way of Glenn's Ferry. The ferryman took the wagons across separately, using the river current to propel the ferry. Each end of the ferry was attached by a rope to a pulley, which ran along a steel cable stretched tightly across the river. The ropes that ran from the ferry to the pulleys were lengthened and shortened as needed to point the bow slightly upstream and the stern slightly downstream. For the return trip, he would not turn the ferry around, but would simply readjust the length of the ropes and let the bow become the stern and the stern the bow as the ferry reversed direction and was again propelled by the force of the river current. It took two trips to take the two sets of horses and wagons across. It was yet another new thing for Jim Henry. He studied the process carefully, wondering at how anyone had thought of it.

———◦———

Jack and Jim Henry paused at the small settlement of Vienna, where a resident obligingly let them use his well to draw water for themselves and their mules. As their mules grazed by the roadside, they pulled thick sandwiches from their vittles boxes and sat in Jack's wagon as they ate.

"In another five miles or so we'll hit the Fayetteville and Western Plank Road," Jack said. "You know it runs all the way from Bethania through Winston and Salem and on to Fayetteville. Some say it is the longest plank road in the world."

Jim Henry had heard about the road all his life. He knew it had taken years to build and had been a wonder, making travel easier and safer and opening up what had been wilderness for farms and towns. He had heard that since the war started, parts of the road had started to fall into disrepair. The men who maintained it were now away, serving in the Confederate Army. Materials that would have gone for the road in peacetime were needed for fighting. And with the advent of railroads, everyone knew the days of the plank roads were numbered. Jim Henry was glad to have a chance to ride on the road while it was still usable.

———◦———

As they neared Winston, the Forsyth County seat a mile north of Salem, the road they were following joined with the plank road. Jim Henry gulped when he saw it. It stood eight or nine inches higher than the ground his wagon's wheels sat on, and it would be easy to break an axle trying to bump up onto it.

"Take it slow," Jack said. "See how the planks are staggered? Your wheels will catch, one at a time, and rise up over the edge."

The wagons creaked and groaned as they mounted, but once they were on the plank road, the going was easy. The surface gave a good ride after the rutted, rocky, sometimes muddy roads Jim

Henry was accustomed to. He felt as if he floated over the land-scape now.

———•———

By evening, they passed through the new chewing and smoking tobacco manufacturing town of Winston and arrived at the nearby Moravian community of Salem, where the plank road gave way to the paved streets of that hundred-year-old settlement. The day had been chilly, but the newness of what he saw and the effort re-quired to drive the team kept Jim Henry warm. Now the bitterness of a cold night set in. He was glad his father planned to stop at the Salem Tavern. Jack had been to the tavern before, selling his whis-key, and his stories were of hot meals and big fireplaces and decent beds, even if shared with other travelers.

Jim Henry wasn't disappointed. The dining room was warm and the plates of pork and cornbread put in front of them smelled almost as good as his mother's food. N.A. Chapin, the proprietor, joined them at their table and greeted Jack. Jack introduced Jim Henry.

Mr. Chapin leaned in Jim Henry's direction and asked, "Do you think your father will sell me some of that whiskey?"

Jim Henry replied, "I expect he would if the price is right."

Mr. Chapin laughed. "Jack, you've got a smart boy here. Where are you heading after you leave Salem?"

"Fayetteville," Jim Henry said.

"Well," said Chapin, "I can't compete with Fayetteville prices, but you won't have much time to sell it and make it back here with the returning traffic on the plank road. Traffic generally flows in one direction at a time. Most folks go down there on Monday through Wednesday and back on Thursday through Saturday, so they don't have to keep pulling two wheels off the road to let on-coming wagons get by. It's a three-day run and if you don't make it back by Saturday night, you'll be pulling off the road a lot. Tell you what—I'm getting mighty low, and I'll make you a fair offer for two of your barrels."

In a few minutes Jack and Mr. Chapin concluded a deal that would lighten each of the wagons by one barrel and provide a hedge in case they had trouble selling in Fayetteville. Jack explained later, he believed in doing business so that both parties made out well, and Mr. Chapin was a friend.

On Monday morning, they rose before dawn and set out at first light, because time was of the essence if they were to get to Fayetteville within three days. On ordinary roads, fifteen miles per day was considered a pretty good haul, and men tended to brag a bit if they made twenty. To cover the remaining 120 miles to Fayetteville in three days, they would need to average forty miles per day. The plank road made it possible, but they would need to keep moving almost constantly from dawn to dusk. Then they needed to do their business in Fayetteville and arrive back in Salem preferably by Saturday night and certainly no later than Sunday, so as to move with the traffic, as Mr. Chapin had explained.

—◆—

Jim Henry was not thinking of the risks of the road or the need to meet a demanding travel schedule. All he could think of was the break from the daily work on the family's 509-acre farm. Every morning at 4:30, Jack called up to the sleeping loft, "All right boys!"

Jim Henry, his brothers Quill, age thirteen, and Bill, age eleven, and the hired man, Jim, pulled on their clothes and went down to the ground floor of their log house. Jack would have already kindled a fire from the banked coals and used a burning splinter to light the oil lantern. The boys split and carried in firewood and brought buckets of water from the spring about two hundred yards down behind the house. Two boys together toted three buckets, one in the middle and one on each side for balance. They then headed for the barn to feed and water the animals, milk the cows, and harness and hitch the mules to wagons, plows, harvesting equipment, harrows, sleds, or hay rakes, depending on the work to be done that day.

Unless Eunice needed eggs to make breakfast, they left the egg-gathering to the younger children. On their return from the barn, Jim Henry, Quill, Bill, and Jim devoured Eunice's generous servings of ham, eggs, corn pone, and red-eye gravy.

As soon as there was enough daylight to see where they were going, they headed for the fields. At noon they came in for another meal of meat, vegetables in season, corn pone, and fresh or dried fruit from the orchard. Then they went back to work in the fields until sunset.

During winter, when there were few crops to work, they cleared land, cut down, split, dried, and sawed up whatever trees they needed for buildings and fences and to stoke the fireplace, the tobacco barn, and the 'stillery for the next year. The winter work schedule was punctuated by episodes of hog-killing and whiskey-making. Each evening they would unhitch the horses, feed and water them and the other animals, and milk the cows. Jim Henry, his brothers, and Jim then stumbled back into the cabin, too exhausted to eat more than a few bites of supper. They were asleep almost before they reached their beds.

The next sound they would hear would be Jack's voice. "All right, boys!"

Jim Henry felt trained and ready for the rigors of the trip, which seemed to offer him a break from farm work and a chance to see something of the world.

By Monday night, with dozens of miles between them and home, he even enjoyed nestling into the straw on his wagon, under quilts his mother had thought to pack for him, and sleeping a deep sleep.

———◆———

On Tuesday and Wednesday, Jim Henry and Jack occasionally pulled their right-hand wheels off the road to accommodate oncoming traffic. Though long-distance haulers tended to abide by the daily one-way custom, local traffic would be going in both directions. Jim Henry noticed that as the plank road approached the sparse small towns along the route, the planked portion would be built along the right side of the roadway so that the generally more heavily laden inbound traffic would have the plank surface and the outgoing traffic would use the unimproved portion of the road. Even for heavier wagons it was better to be on an unimproved road for a short distance than to have to constantly drive on and off the plank portion.

Despite all this, Jack and Jim Henry averaged forty miles per day for three days. After spending two nights in campgrounds crowded with fellow travelers, they arrived in Fayetteville, passed the central marketplace, and between there and the Cape Fear River found a small tavern with accommodations for them, their mules, and wagons.

As they sat down to supper at the tavern, Jack asked a lengthy blessing, in which he praised the Lord for his faithfulness to them and thanked Him for bringing them and their cargo safely to Fayetteville and for the good meal before them. He finally asked the Lord to bless the meal they were about to receive and to give them good rest for tomorrow.

Jack said to Jim Henry, "We've been mighty fortunate on this trip. The road from home to Winston is often impassable in winter, and that freeze made it hard as pavement. Then look how far we have come on this plank road in only four days, and for tolls amounting to less than five dollars."

The next morning, they drove their wagons to the public market in the center of town. The market building stood three stories tall, including the clock tower on top. Jim Henry was impressed by the size of the buildings in Fayetteville, the largest city in North Carolina. Jack asked someone where he should go to sell his whiskey. They were directed to an area in the market where distillers and their customers met and made their deals. Within an hour, Jack had sold all four barrels of whiskey at a good price. Then he and Jim Henry shopped among the stalls for provisions for the trip home. There was quite a selection of fresh pork, cured ham, mutton, veal, venison, poultry, fish, cheese, butter, lard, eggs, vegetables, dried fruits, meal, corn, peas, oats, and the like.

Jim Henry had no part to play in his father's bargaining and negotiating, so even though he knew he could learn a lot, he was drawn to explore on his own. He heard a loud voice announcing a public sale, saw other people move toward it, and followed the crowd.

He moved between people until he reached the front and had a clear view. A young negro woman stood on a platform, three children around her. She grasped their hands as best she could, bent down to whisper to them. The oldest child, a boy Jim Henry took to be five or six years old, whimpered and held his mother's skirt. A man, his hands bound, stood to the side, his face twisted as if in agony, but when he moved as if to go to the woman, a white man blocked his way and threatened him with a club.

Another white man stepped forward and began to call out, "We got a fine family here. You buy these young'uns now, while they go cheap, and before you know it, they'll double their value."

Jim Henry had been to livestock auctions with his father, and he'd heard calves described this way. He had felt sorry for both calf and cow when they were sold separately and bawled for each other long after they were led in opposite directions and out of sight. Now, when no one made an offer for the family, the auctioneer motioned for the man to be shoved forward and asked, "Who'll open the bidding for this strong, healthy field hand?"

Jim Henry had heard his teacher, the Reverend John Bond, expound on the horrors of slavery. He had read Harriet Beecher Stowe's Uncle Tom's Cabin and remembered the scene in which a slave mother saw her child being sold away from her. His own father had freed the only slave he ever had as soon as the slave came into his possession. Jim was ten years old when he had been left to Jack by his uncle Henry. Once freed, Jim stayed with the Shore family and grew up working on the farm as a hired hand.

Jim Henry had seen slaves working in the fields, but never had he seen any abuse. He had never observed or heard about slaves being bought and sold in Yadkin County. Even though his mother and the reverend spoke against it, slavery had never seemed dire to Jim Henry. Now, watching the auction, he began to feel a deep chill.

The father of the slave family was sold. The auctioneer began to sell the children separately to different buyers over the sobs of the weeping mother. Jim Henry's eyes were drawn to her, and for a moment they made direct eye contact as she appeared to plead for intervention. He thought of the proceeds from the whiskey sales, and even started to go through the math, but realized it would not be nearly enough to buy the whole family. A rage welled up within him. It was small comfort to him that the same person who bought the mother also bought the youngest child.

Suddenly the image of Jesse Dobbins flashed into Jim Henry's mind, and he sensed that the time was coming when he himself would have to make the hard decision between obeying the conscription law and going north. If the war lasted another year, he'd be faced with that choice.

In any event, he knew he had no use for slavery or the Confederacy.

Even over the auctioneer's ringing voice and the calls from the crowd, Jim Henry heard his dad's shrill whistle. He wasn't sorry to have an excuse to leave the scene behind.

3

Homeward

$\mathcal{J}$ack and Jim Henry headed toward the riverfront and found the office and warehouse facility where they could pick up part of Yadkin County's allocation of salt. The precious commodity was produced under state contract in furnaces along the sounds near Wilmington. Upon presenting his commission from the Yadkin County commissioners, Jack purchased forty sacks of salt at a price based upon the state's cost.

Each sack contained three bushels, or 150 pounds, of salt. A total of 3,000 pounds in each wagon was as much as Jack felt they could carry without too much risk of breakdown. After the salt was loaded, they headed west on Yadkin Road and soon picked up the Fayetteville and Western Plank Road, beginning the journey home.

It was midday on Thursday, February 5, so they could not hope to complete the three-day journey to Salem by Saturday. They hoped to encounter light traffic on Sunday, but travelers would be going in both directions.

In order to get as far as possible on Thursday, they did not stop until dusk. There was no campground nearby, and they simply pulled off the road at a farmhouse and gained permission to draw water from a well and spend the night in a field adjacent to the road. As they dined on the provisions they had acquired, Jim Henry told Jack what he had seen at the auction.

"I couldn't believe it, Dad. No bidder was willing to buy the whole family, so the husband and two older children were sold to three different men, and the mother and baby were sold to a fourth. I thought the cries of desperation would never stop as the slaves were led off by their new owners. How can anyone be for slavery?"

Jack responded, "You are just seeing a pitiful, but rare, situation. Never have I heard of such a situation in Yadkin County, where even slaves are usually treated with respect."

"But Dad," Jim Henry said, "should the law ever allow such disrespect of slaves and their families?"

Jack diverted the conversation from this uncomfortable subject by saying, "Well, that's certainly something to think about."

Jim Henry wasn't satisfied. "But what can we do to stop the mistreatment I saw today?"

"Nothing, son. There are some things you and I can't change. This thing is just going to have to play itself out."

——◆——

They made good time on Friday and Saturday, but on Sunday, just when they thought they would have a short day's run into Salem, they began to encounter problems. Jim Henry and Jack had to drop their right-hand wheels off the planks to let eastbound wagons pass. As they remounted the plank road, their wheels caught one of the staggered planks and groaned under the stress. Eventually, the right front wheel of Jim Henry's wagon lost its rigidity and the iron tire began to loosen from the wheel. They stopped several times to repair the wheel and to nail and tie the tire in place. Each time the repairs were short-lived and eventually the wheel collapsed. With help from passers-by, they removed some of the load and moved the disabled wagon to the side of the road.

Fortunately, they were within a few miles of Waughtown and the Nissen Wagon Works, which had manufactured their wagons.

The wagon works was operating under contract with the Confederate government to supply wagons and gun carts for the war effort, and Jack hoped that they might find someone at the facility, even on Sunday.

Jack flagged down a passing teamster. "We have broken a wheel. Would you please take my son and the broken wheel to the Nissen Wagon Works just ahead to get it fixed?"

The teamster nodded toward Jim Henry. "Just put your wheel in the back and hop in."

Jim Henry was happy to play an active role in the transaction while Jack stayed behind to secure the wagon.

The Nissen Wagon Works were closed, but Jim Henry was able to find Mr. J.P. Nissen at his home, not far away.

"Mr. Nissen," Jim Henry said, "I'm Jim Henry Shore. My father's Jack Shore. I believe you know him. He is on the side of the road a few miles east of here with two wagons of salt and two teams of mules. Is there any way you can fix this wheel for us?"

"Son," Mr. Nissen said, "that wheel is beyond repair, although we may be able to salvage some of the parts. You need an entirely new wheel. Because of our heavy commitments for military production, we'll have to work it in sometime over the next two days."

Jim Henry knew his dad didn't want to wait that long. "Could you possibly do it in one day, sir?"

"We're busy with war work. I wouldn't even undertake a minor repair like this, if it wasn't one of our own wheels that broke. It has seen a lot of use, but still should not have failed like that."

Mr. Nissen promised to have the wheel delivered to the breakdown site on Wednesday. Jim Henry hitched a ride on a wagon headed east to rejoin his father. As soon as Jim Henry had dismounted from the wagon and thanked his benefactor, his father introduced him to a farmer who lived nearby and who had invited them to join his family for dinner.

Upon learning they would be delayed for two days and that their provisions were running low, the farmer offered to board Jack and Jim Henry if they would help him clear some new ground. The next two days, Monday and Tuesday, Jack and Jim Henry cut trees, pulled stumps, and cleared brush to create a new field where the farmer could plant tobacco seeds. It was something they were used to doing on their own farm. Tobacco seeds would grow much better in the rich topsoil of newly cleared woods than in a previously cultivated field. The farmer was grateful and gave them generous supplies of food and fodder for their animals.

On Wednesday, a man from the wagon works delivered the new wheel and helped Jack and Jim Henry install it. Because eastbound traffic flooded the plank road, they had to stay on the dirt part of the road as they moved to the northwest. As a result, they made poor time. The sky was turning dark and they were encountering snow flurries by the time they reached the Salem Tavern. Mr. Chapin greeted them with a smile, and its warmth was accompanied by the warmth of the fireplaces throughout the tavern. Jack and Jim Henry thanked the Lord for their safe return to the last place they had slept in a bed.

On Thursday, February 12, Jack and Jim Henry fed and hitched up their horses, ate a hearty breakfast, and left at first light for Yadkin County by way of Glenn's Ferry. As they drove through the bottomlands up toward the Glenwood mansion, they saw slaves cutting wood and dragging it by mule to a yard, where other slaves were sawing and splitting it for fuel.

They drove by the Williams farm. Jim Henry wished he could see Julia for just five minutes, maybe get another kiss, but he knew better than to ask. His dad would push on, in a hurry now to get the salt to its destination and to be back home.

With the heavy loads of salt in their wagons and the fresh dusting of snow on the ground, Jim Henry and Jack's progress was slow, and the sun was about to set as they reached the John Shore farm. John and his wife, Susanna, greeted their son and grandson with joy, added to the supper already being prepared, and summoned their nearby relatives. Jim Henry told his grandparents, aunts, uncles, and cousins about the trip to Fayetteville, which none of them had ever seen.

On a chilly but clear Friday morning, February 13, Jack and Jim Henry set out for their home some ten miles to the west. By three o'clock that afternoon they were less than a mile from the Deep Creek Friends Meeting House when they heard volley after volley of gunfire straight ahead. The gunfire subsided, and they proceeded cautiously in its direction.

As they drew closer to the church, they could see that the shooting was taking place at the Bond School located on the Deep Creek church property. Jack stopped his wagon and waved for Jim Henry to come alongside.

Jim Henry said, "I bet that's Jesse and his group going north. It sounds like they may be in trouble. Maybe we can help them."

"Make sure your rifle is where you can reach it—we're going over there," Jack said.

The shooting had stopped, but as they neared the school, Jim Henry held his rifle across his knees. He looked toward the building and a man in a militia uniform stared back at him. Jim Henry recognized the man as James West, captain of the militia. It was odd to see somebody he knew as a peaceful man, a man respected by all, in warlike circumstances.

Captain West turned and walked up to the door of the school, took another glance at Jack and Jim Henry, then banged on the door and began shouting and cursing. The door opened, two shots rang out in quick succession, and the militia man fell right in front of the door. Both sides exchanged gunfire, and in a few moments another man Jim Henry recognized, John Williams, appeared to take charge as leader of the militia. There was no let-up in the battle, and Captain Williams fell dead.

The militiamen fell back, as they needed time to reload their muzzle loaders. With both their leaders down, Jim Henry saw disorder and confusion among them.

A voice from within the schoolhouse shouted, "Let's go!" and several men came out through the door and a side window and ran behind the schoolhouse. Jesse Dobbins led them as they rounded the corner, out of sight, except for one man, who fell wounded just outside the door. Jack and Jim Henry watched as the militiamen moved out of their covered positions behind trees and fences, gathered their two lifeless comrades, tied them belly down across their own saddles, and rode away.

Jack and Jim Henry jumped down from their wagons and ran to the schoolhouse. The wounded man was named Eck Allgood. He lived some distance away, but they knew him well. He was still alive, but very weak.

Inside the building, they found another friend and neighbor, Sol Hinshaw, motionless in a pool of blood, a large bullet hole in the place on his chest where they ordinarily might have listened for a heartbeat.

"We can't help him, son," Jack said. "Let's see if we can help Eck."

As they went back out, neighbors began to arrive. Among the first was Jesse's wife, Catharine Dobbins, who came running up from their house a short distance south on Rockford Road. She ran to the fallen Eck Allgood, cradled his head in her lap, and asked, "What happened to Jesse?" In a weak voice, Eck said, "He got away clean, along with my brother Horace and almost all the others. Sol Hinshaw is dead. Two others are wounded."

Lydia Bond, wife of John Bond, III, Reverend Bond's grandson, lived a short distance to the north on Rockford Road. She came running. When she saw that Jack and Jim Henry had wagons, she said, "Jack, put Eck in your wagon and take him to my house where I can attend to him."

Jack said, "That will be fine, and Jim Henry here can take Sol Hinshaw's body to his home." Jack and Jim Henry spread their bedding on top of the salt bags, and loving friends helped load the dead Sol Hinshaw and nearly dead Eck Allgood onto the wagons and accompanied them to their destinations.

After making their separate deliveries, Jack and Jim Henry reached home at almost the same time. Eunice, the children, and Jim the farm hand came running to see them. As she hugged Jack, Eunice said, "I was worried about you. We've heard about the shooting at the school. Where have you been?"

Jim Henry was exhausted, and now that he was home, he saw the trip fade in significance compared with the horrible violence they had just seen.

Jack answered "Jesse and his boys didn't get away quick enough. They stayed in the Bond School waiting for the weather to get better. The militia learned they were there and came after them. Sol Hinshaw is dead and Eck Allgood is just barely hanging on. At least most of them got away. Jim West, the militia captain and his fellow officer, John Williams, were killed. There was a lot of blood shed for no good reason."

That night as he said his prayers, Jim Henry thought about what his father had said and what he had seen in Fayetteville. Was there any good reason for what happened? Was there any good reason for the war? Slavery was not worth defending, but wasn't it all right to defend your own state from being occupied by an invading army? Did the Lord have a purpose in it? If so, what?

4
Yadkinville

*J*im Henry had been eager to tell his brothers everything he'd seen on the trip. And he'd looked forward to his own bed and his mother's good cooking. But the joy of homecoming was chilled by the shootout at the Bond School. Any remaining joy was quenched that afternoon when a deputy sheriff rode to the farm and handed Jack a subpoena requiring him to appear in the county courthouse the next afternoon and give testimony as to whether those in the schoolhouse should be arrested for first-degree murder.

Jim Henry stood beside his dad as Jack told the deputy, "I don't want to testify against those boys."

The deputy replied, "That will be up to Solicitor Armfield."

Early the next morning, Jim Henry took food his mother had prepared to Lydia Bond's house. By some miracle, Eck Allgood had survived the night. Weak and in great pain, Eck looked directly at Jim Henry and said, "Don't do what I did. It just isn't worth it."

Minutes later, Eck drew his last breath.

Jim Henry was shaken by Eck's last words. The war was not a philosophical issue anymore. It was a matter of life and death, not only for others, but for himself.

———◆———

Jim Henry hurried home to tell the news, and within minutes he was heading to court in Yadkinville with Jack. They drove one of the wagons still loaded with the salt they had brought from

Fayetteville. They unloaded it at the county manager's office, then headed for court.

They had to walk through a crowd of people gathered outside the courthouse. Men were drinking and passing around whiskey jugs. A man stood in a wagon bed and made a speech in opposition to the militia killing people in furtherance of the Confederate conscription law. Most of the listeners cheered him, but a few yelled their support for the Confederacy. Jim Henry hoped there would not be more violence, not with him as an onlooker.

Inside the packed courtroom, the atmosphere was deadly serious. Militia members and their supporters filled the seats. The judge was on the bench, and Solicitor Armfield was making his case for the warrant by testimony of some of the militiamen. He did not call Jack as a witness.

As soon as he had heard the evidence, the justice of the peace, T.L. Tulbert, signed a lengthy arrest warrant, charging Jesse Dobbins and the other men who had survived the shootout at the school with the murders of James West and John Williams.

As people stood up to leave the courtroom, Jim Henry spotted Mr. Wade Williams and ran to greet him.

As they shook hands, Jim Henry got right to the point, "How is Julia?"

"She is with her mother right now over at the store."

"Thanks, I'll try to see her."

Jim Henry took hasty leave of Mr. Williams and told Jack he would be back in a little while. He sprinted across the road to the dry goods store of which Mr. Williams was part owner. As he burst through the door, he saw Julia and she saw him. She joined him in an embrace. He saw her mother's shocked face, but for that minute, did not care. All he knew was that Julia still loved him.

"Will you take a walk with me?" he asked her. "I want to tell you what's happened."

He led Julia outside. A crowd of men had gathered in front

of the courthouse. The crowd was unruly and some were drunk. As Jim Henry and Julia made their way through, one of the young men put an unwelcome hand on her. Jim Henry knocked it away and faced him down. Jim Henry was the smaller of the two, but he felt ten feet tall in his anger. The other youth decided that the issue was not worth taking on a determined attacker and slunk off.

To get out of the cold, they went into another store on the opposite side of the street and pretended to look at merchandise, but with their eyes fixed mostly on each other. They found a corner where they were alone and could talk.

Jim Henry told her about his trip to Fayetteville. He had to pinch himself so he didn't cry as he told her about the sale of the slave family and the killings at the Bond School. Julia was shaken by the story of the slave family being split up and sold.

"Slaves are treated worse in Fayetteville than around here," she said. "My father buys and sells slaves, but never in such a cruel manner. He has been very busy settling one of our relative's estate. He's running the entire farming operation, so now our family is responsible for a property that is not even ours. He says he is dependent on slavery and that influences him into support of the Confederacy."

Jim Henry felt himself to be on shaky ground. The last thing he wanted was to argue with Julia.

"My father," he said, "has to travel a lot to bring salt to Yadkin County, and the loss of Jesse Dobbins means that I will need to take his place. We may go back to Fayetteville, and in the spring, once the roads into the mountains are passable, we'll go to Virginia for salt. It will be difficult for us to see much of each other."

Julia looked up at Jim, her face painted with sorrow. "It has already been difficult," she confessed. "It seems that it has been near impossible for us to see each other, even now. Is there any alternative?"

"None, except to join the Confederate Army, which still may

be a possibility since pulling a wagon to transport salt does not defer me from the draft. My family does not want me to fight, but once I am old enough, I fear that I may not have a choice except to go north and perhaps serve in the Union Army."

Julia looked longingly at him. "You can't fight for the North, Jim Henry. My family wouldn't accept that. You know my brother Lewis died in the army. He was brave and prepared for combat, but he died from disease before he ever saw battle. I hope brother Lewis did not die in vain."

She began to cry a little, and Jim Henry put his arms around her. Then she said, "I love you, and I always will."

"I love you. I love you forever. The war will not stand between us. And one day, we'll make a life together."

5
Losses

Jim Henry knew that when Julia spoke of her brother Lewis, she was serious. When he died while serving the Confederacy, word spread throughout the county. Jim Henry's own mother had wept for the loss of a young man she had known as a child. She spoke of how difficult it must be for Mrs. Williams to have had a son die in such a way. But Jim Henry was aware of how differently the two families saw the war. To Julia and the Williamses, if the South lost the war, Lewis's death was in vain. To Eunice, the death of thousands of promising young men was proof of how awful war was.

At the time the war began, Lewis Williams was Jim Henry's teacher at the Bond School. The school's founder, Reverend John Bond, was a highly respected teacher who instilled Biblical and Quaker values in his students. He preached against slavery and the use of alcoholic beverages. When Abraham Lincoln was elected president in 1860, Reverend Bond foresaw that war would be the result. He was then in his eighties and decided to retire. He moved to Indiana to be near his family.

It was then that Lewis Williams was hired to replace him. The Quakers of Deep Creek had forced the Williams family to move because of their ownership of slaves and their belief that slaves should not be educated at the Bond School, but Lewis was an adult and was considered to be emancipated from his family. Jim Henry had hoped that Julia would be permitted to attend the

Bond School, but at age fourteen she still lived with her parents so was judged by their slaveholding, as well as their residency outside of the school district.

The Union Army attacked Fort Sumter soon after the school year ended in 1861, and that inspired Lewis to join the Confederate Army. He was assigned to build the fortifications around Fort Fisher near Wilmington, North Carolina, and soon contracted measles, which ultimately led to his death.

The Shore family had known its share of loss. Jim Henry's namesake uncle was only twenty-seven when he died. Since Jim Henry was a young child at the time, he had no memories of him. He did have memories of the babies his mother had given birth to, who had died.

The first death was of an infant sister on August 6, 1855. Jim Henry recalled watching his father's eyes moisten as he made a small casket for her.

Her funeral was held in their grassy yard beneath the shade of young black walnut trees Jack had planted. After the preaching, family and friends partook in a big dinner prepared by Eunice and some of her many friends. Jim Henry remembered the children all having a good time, but when they all went home, he still had a sad feeling of loss.

Jim Henry lost two more sisters in 1859. On March 21, his sister Susan died at the age of two and a half years, and ten days later his sister Margaret died at the age of five months.

Wade and Annie Williams and several of their children, including Julia, attended the single funeral held for both girls. When Jim Henry saw them arriving in their buggy, he ran to greet Julia and her family and to help Wade unhitch the horses and turn them into the nearby pasture. During the preaching he sat with his family, but as soon as it was over, he made a beeline toward Julia. She met him halfway across the yard.

They walked hand-in-hand down the path that led through

the woods to the spring. When they reached the spring, Jim Henry looked around. They were alone. He held out his arms, both afraid and certain of her response. She moved toward him and they hugged. It was a cold day, so they huddled together and whispered to each other.

"I miss you so much," he said.

"It's not fair that we can't see each other. My mother makes me so mad."

They heard Wade Williams calling, "Julia, we're leaving."

They walked together from the spring back toward the house. Julia looked at Jim Henry. "I know your father depends on you to help work the farm, but please try to find a way to come and see me, maybe on a Sunday. My parents won't let me come see you."

Jim Henry lost two more siblings at birth, and their funerals were small family affairs. An infant was stillborn on August 3, 1860, and another daughter was born and died on March 31, 1866. Jack and Eunice Shore buried the five of their children who did not survive early childhood in a small family cemetery on a corner of the family farm.

When Julia spoke about her dead brother, Jim Henry could share the sense of loss. What he could not bear was to think of losing her.

6

Jim Henry's Dilemma

The funeral of the young and promising Lewis Williams in 1861 had been a sad occasion, but it gave Jim Henry a chance to see Julia. When she entered the small church with her family, her face was solemn and wet with tears, and to Jim Henry, more beautiful than ever.

Following the funeral and the burial service in the cemetery just outside the church, Jim Henry found Julia, and once they were alone, they hugged each other warmly. She began sobbing and could hardly speak. Jim Henry tried to console her.

"I wish I could see you more often," he said.

"Please come. I need you, Jim Henry."

"It's ten miles, Julia. Dad needs me on the farm every day."

"Ten miles doesn't sound like a lot, not when we love each other so much." She wiped away tears and rested her head on his shoulder. "You know how to get to your grandparents' house, don't you?"

"Sure I do," he said.

"If you keep going past their farm about halfway to the Glenwood mansion, the road passes the farm where we live. Look for a white house on the left. You cannot miss it. Please find a way."

That night at supper Jim Henry told his family of his interest in seeing Julia and how near to his grandparents she lived. He suggested that it would be nice for the family to see his grandparents. He caught the look that passed between his mother and father, and his mother's little smile.

The very next Sunday, the family climbed into the wagon and went to visit Jack's parents, John and Susannah Shore, and Jim Henry's aunts, uncles, and cousins who lived near them.

Shortly after their arrival, Jim Henry slipped away on foot to see Julia.

From the warmth of her hug and kiss, Jim Henry could tell that Julia was overjoyed at his surprise visit. Her parents also came to the door to greet him and ushered everyone into the parlor. Much to Jim Henry's disappointment, he and Julia had little opportunity to be alone. Julia's large family was all over the house, and the February cold did not lend itself to walking outdoors. Her parents treated Jim Henry with a formal respect, which kept him at a certain distance. He was aware that they didn't share Julia's enthusiasm for his visit, but he knew that they were meant for each other and somehow parents' approval didn't matter. He and Julia would find a way to be together.

——◆——

On his fifteenth birthday, February 20, 1862, Jim Henry's parents gave him a colt, which he broke to a saddle and trained as a buggy horse. The colt was black as coal except for a white diamond on the front of his head between his nose and forehead. Jim Henry named him "Coalie." Jim Henry then began visiting Julia on Sunday afternoons, as often as possible. As time went on, Julia's parents allowed them to take horseback rides together. Once well out of sight of the house and family, the rides turned into walks, and when the opportunity presented itself, they shared tight embraces and many kisses. They knew they were already beyond the social conventions of the day and dared go no further.

In spite of their willingness to trust Jim Henry with their daughter, Julia's parents seemed to be very formal in their relationship with him. He sensed it was not a matter of not liking him. He began to think it might have had something to do with the slavery issue and their hurt at being shunned by people at Deep Creek.

Finally, he perceived that what distanced Julia's parents from him was the war, a war for which their son had given his life. They knew his parents were opposed to the war, and maybe they wondered where Jim Henry stood on it. If so, they were not alone, because Jim Henry was not sure either. He began to consider whether he would ever fight for the Confederacy. He felt he might one day be caught between two bad choices, either supporting a dubious cause or breaking the conscription law. There was no way to please both her family and his. Maybe the war would end before he had to make a choice.

7
Saltville

On the first of May 1863, Jack and Jim Henry worked in the pre-dawn darkness to load their vittles boxes, put hay and quilts in their wagons, and hitch their teams for their first trip to Saltville in Virginia together. Whenever Jack got home from one of the journeys he and Jesse Dobbins had made, he told stories of the twists and turns of the mountains and the splashes from the rivers. Jim Henry felt like he knew exactly where he was going because Jack's stories were so vivid. At first light, they headed north on Rockford Road, which led to the shallows where they could ford the Yadkin River. The river was noticeably narrower here than at Glenn's Ferry some twenty miles downstream. They passed the small village of Rockford and headed for the Surry County seat of Dobson, where they camped for the night.

The next day, as he drove Jack's old wagon drawn by Jesse's two mules, Jim Henry was glad that their wagons were not loaded with whiskey or anything else. The road they climbed was steep and rocky to the top of the escarpment at Low Gap. Jack cautioned him about how to use his brakes to avoid damaging the wagons or the teams.

They gained some two thousand feet in elevation that day and the mules were exhausted as they stopped and camped for the night on the eastern edge of the Blue Ridge.

On the third day, as they drove their wagons along the plateau just beyond the escarpment, the terrain became much more level

VIEW OF SALTVILLE, VIRGINIA.

During the Civil War, Saltville's salt mines were crucial in enabling the Confederacy to preserve meat and process leather. Engraving from the January 14, 1865, issue of Harper's Weekly.

and the road improved. It improved even more when it descended into the valleys first of the Chestnut River and then of the New River, which Jack said flowed from North Carolina to Virginia and became the Kanawa River as it entered West Virginia on its way to the Ohio and Mississippi Rivers. They camped that night where the Chestnut River flows into the New River near Fries Junction.

The next morning, they continued along the New River, crossed it at Jackson's Ferry, which was water-driven like the one at Glenn's Ferry. It was larger and easily accommodated the two wagons and their teams.

At Fort Chiswell, they changed their northwesterly course through the mountains to a southwesterly course down the Valley of Virginia. The road flattened and was free of rocks, so they covered well over twenty miles that day. They spent that night at a wagon camp just outside of Wytheville. Jack explained to Jim Henry what he had learned on previous trips to Saltville, that in prehistoric times, the valleys between the newly formed ridges of the Blue Ridge had no outlet to the sea and, as water accumulated and evaporated, salt accumulated first in lakes and then in the soil when the lakes dried up.

"Any of these lakes left?" asked Jim Henry.

"The lakes are gone. Only thing left is the salt in the ground. Guess it would have been like the Great Salt Lake or the Dead Sea around here if the water had not found a way to break out."

The next day as they drove southwest along the Valley of Virginia, Jim Henry saw that most of the land had been cleared. At home, flat land was cleared for crops and pasture and hilly land was left forested. Here, even hills were cleared for pasture. As they ate their supper that night at a wagon camp near Marion, Jim Henry commented on the scarcity of trees.

Jack responded, "Every state in the Confederacy owns furnaces or has contracted for the production of salt furnaces in Saltville. The amount of wood consumed by those many furnaces has caused all the timber to be cut and burned for miles around Saltville. I see now the cut-over areas extend much further than they did last fall. We are still about twenty miles out."

"I saw people selling firewood along the road. Do you think we could make money by buying firewood here and selling it in Saltville?"

"Not a bad idea, son."

The next morning, they stopped and bought firewood from a roadside vendor and loaded their wagons. The extra weight hardly slowed their trip through the Valley of Virginia, although it did slow them down a bit as they turned toward the northwest and crossed a ridge to reach the small valley where Saltville lay.

However, they could not have gone much faster anyway because of the dense wagon traffic. Jack said that there were five roads leading into Saltville with a total of about a thousand wagons a day.

As they drove into town, the Palmer Hotel looked inviting to Jim Henry, but Jack chose to continue their habit of camping. They found a place to park their wagons and tie their horses near the North Carolina furnaces. They looked for Mr. Woodfin, North Carolina's agent for salt purchases. Mr. Woodfin was not present, but through his assistant they made arrangements to sell their wood and pick up their salt the next morning. Because of their load of wood, they slept under the wagons rather than in them.

The next morning, Jack and Jim Henry unloaded the wood and loaded as much salt as they could carry. Jim Henry wanted to see how the salt was produced. Mr. Woodfin's assistant showed them the pumps that injected water into the ground and brought the salt-laden water back up. He then showed them the North Carolina furnaces where the water was boiled down until only dry salt remained. It was then bagged for shipping by wagon or by railway car.

The trip back home was accomplished in a week. Jack's and Jim Henry's wagons were fully loaded, which meant they slept on the ground and had to pull hard on their brakes as they went downhill, especially as they descended the steep escarpment at Low Gap.

Jim Henry thought often of Julia and how soon he would be able to tell her about all he had seen and learned. On the last evening as they pulled onto the farm, Jack and Jim Henry, let out joyful whoops to let Eunice and the family know they were home and hungry.

8

Duty

On January 5, 1864, the Confederate Congress enacted a law to decrease the minimum conscription age from eighteen to seventeen years and to increase the maximum age from forty-five to fifty years. The effect of the law was to make Jim Henry eligible for conscription the following month instead of the following year, as his seventeenth birthday was February 20. He still hoped for exemption because of his work with his father in the salt trade.

Then on February 17, 1864, the conscription law was further changed to limit such exemptions. Although it did not mention salt workers by name, the new law restricted the governor's power to exempt government contractors unless the government department making the contract certified that the personal services of the contractor were indispensable to the execution of the contract. It further specified that those exempted from military service be at least forty-five years of age. Jack was old enough to qualify for the salt agent exemption, but Jim Henry was a minor and could not enter into a valid contract because he was not yet twenty-one.

The same rule was applicable to the freed man, Jim. There was no exemption for free African Americans, thousands of whom served in the Confederate Army, many in non-combat roles such as cooking, but there were also many who served in combat units.

The Shore household waited with dread to see what would happen to two beloved members. To add to the drama, the courts got involved.

Neither Jim Henry nor Jim had to report for duty immediately because of rulings by Chief Justice Richmond Pearson. In addition to serving as chief justice of the three-judge North Carolina Supreme Court, he served as resident superior court judge in Yadkin County. He granted numerous writs of habeas corpus to young conscripts who wished to contest the Confederate conscription laws. To counter Judge Pearson, the Confederate Congress passed an act suspending the writ of habeas corpus.

Then on February 29, 1864, the North Carolina Supreme Court held that the suspension of the writ of habeas corpus applied only to criminal cases and not to cases of conscription.

However, on May 22, 1864, a majority of the court, under pressure from the Confederate government and Governor Zebulon Baird Vance, outvoted Pearson and held that the writ of habeas corpus was no longer available to conscripts. The court also upheld the Confederate law wiping out a previous exemption for those who hired a substitute soldier and requiring such people to serve.

The outcome of this case made it obvious that conscripts had no chance for legal recourse at the hand of Chief Justice Pearson. Jim Henry and Jim now faced a decision to obey the conscription law or flee to avoid prosecution.

Jim Henry's immediate family and most of their friends in the Deep Creek Meeting did not want him to serve in the Confederate Army. Jim Henry's mother often spoke of how her grandfather, Abraham Reece, had operated a thousand-acre farm without slave labor, and it was her view that others should do likewise.

Jack's side of the family had come from Virginia for the purpose of settling in the Moravian community of Bethabara, North Carolina. The Moravian Church owned the farmland surrounding the town as well as a number of slaves who helped the residents work the land. The church's position was that private ownership of slaves was not permissible because of the possibility of mistreatment, and that by owning the slaves itself, it could see to it that they were treated well.

Bethabara had a sufficient population to serve the community's needs, and the church started a new community in Bethania, a few miles to the northwest. The new church and settlement needed more people. The Shore family—Jack's father and mother—had no strong church connections of any kind at the time, so they joined the Moravian Church in order to receive an allocation of land in Bethania. When Jack moved away from Bethania to settle in Yadkin County, he left the Moravian Church and had no church affiliation. However, like the Moravian Church, he had no compunctions against slavery as long as slaves were treated well. He knew enough not to take on Eunice on this issue, and he had offered no resistance to Eunice's suggestion that Jim be given his freedom. Jim Henry was aware of how his parents differed on slavery, and that his mother's opinion prevailed at home.

Although Jack read his Bible regularly and took his family to the neighborhood Reece Church almost every Sunday, neither he nor Eunice formally joined that church. The Reece Church was loosely affiliated with the Southern Baptist denomination, which had split from the American Baptist denomination over the issue of slavery. Eunice had become a member of Deep Creek Friends Meeting as a child and maintained her affiliation. As a young man, Jim Henry attended Reece Church and occasionally the Friends Meeting, but also felt that church membership was not necessary to a strong faith.

It was natural for Jim Henry to inherit and maintain a bit of skepticism about churches. His great-great-grandfather had left the Reformed Protestant Church in Muttenz, Switzerland, in 1750 to come to North America. Church records reflected the following journal entry: "Hans Frederick Schor left several months ago. We don't know whether he will return, as some think he went to the New World, but it doesn't make much difference because he never gave much money to the church anyway." This entry was translated by the family as a message of "good riddance." Jim Henry had heard this story many times, as told by his grandfather and father.

Jim Henry suspected the "good riddance" went both ways, and that if his ancestor had had adequate money, he would not have left Switzerland in the first place.

Jim Henry sometimes wondered whether churches were truly righteous. If the Moravian Church was truly righteous in forbidding its members to own slaves, then how could the church follow its practice of owning slaves itself, and then renting them out to its members? More particularly, he wondered how the Quaker Deep Creek Church could take its position on slavery to the point of punishing an innocent schoolgirl like Julia. Why wouldn't the church honor the last part of Deuteronomy where Moses said the child should not be punished for the sin of the father?

The Williams family's loss of a son and brother and their disdain for those who did not serve were some of the currents that kept Jim Henry's decision from being an easy one. He wanted Julia's approval, and that of her father.

Like most North Carolinians, Jim Henry had no interest in preserving slavery, but he did have an interest in home, family, and neighbors. Northern troops had already invaded and occupied parts of eastern North Carolina and Tennessee. There was a constant fear of Union raids from Tennessee into western North Carolina. He had an abiding interest in defending his homeland from invasion.

There was also the practical consideration that military service was the lesser of several evils, when the alternatives were facing arrest, hiding out as Jesse and others had done, or crossing the lines to the North. He remembered what he had seen at the Bond School, with two neighbors dead and others at war with each other.

From his seventeenth birthday on February 20 until his enlistment on June 23, 1864, Jim Henry wrestled and prayed about all these considerations. In the final analysis, it came down to whether these inclinations were more in line with the preferences of his mother or those of his sweetheart, and whether or not he was prepared to become an outlaw.

On the eve of his enlistment in the Confederate army, Jim Henry rode to the Wade Williams home early in the morning to say his last good-byes. It was a weekday, so Julia and her mother were the only ones at home. Although Julia was apprehensive about him going to war, her mother was most supportive of the decision he had made. Jim Henry seized the opportunity to ask if Julia would like to go for a walk, and Annie did not object. In a moment they were out the door and headed off across the large farm in the direction of pasture and woods rather than cropland where work was going on. On reaching a secluded meadow, Jim Henry stopped Julia under a large oak tree and said, "I love you so much!"

She responded with the same words she had spoken on the field trip at the one-room school seven years earlier, "I love you, Jim Henry!"

Jim Henry drew her to him in a strong embrace. She wrapped one arm around his back and the other around his neck and they kissed deeply. Julia drew back, looked into his eyes and said, "Please keep yourself safe. It was hard enough to lose my brother Lewis, and I would die if I lost you."

"You need not worry about my trying to be safe. How could I risk losing a chance to spend the rest of my life with you?"

They walked back to the house together. Jim Henry spoke to Annie, who said, "May the Lord watch over you and bring you home safe." Julia said a loud, "Amen!"

Jim Henry mounted his horse and did not look back at Julia. He did not want to chance seeing her crying.

—◆—

On the day of his enlistment, Jim Henry left home as soon as the early chores were done. Jack gave him a wagon ride to Yadkinville, where Jim Henry lined up in front of the courthouse at eight a.m. and enlisted in the Confederate Army. He and the other conscripts, mostly seventeen-year-olds, spent the next ten hours or more walking some thirty-eight miles to Camp Fisher, a Confederate camp and military training facility near Salisbury. When they arrived, hungry and exhausted, they were given food and bedding for the night.

The next morning, the commanding officer of Camp Fisher called the new arrivals into formation and announced that those less than eighteen years of age were considered junior reserves and would receive their training and perform prison-guard duty at Camp Vance, eighty miles to the west and five miles from Morganton. He then announced that those forty-five years old or older were considered to be senior reserves and would be assigned to the nearby Salisbury Prison for training and guard duty. He explained that these categories had been created to keep those who had recently become liable for conscription away from the front lines.

Each soldier was issued a knapsack, one pair of trousers called jeans, a long-sleeved battle shirt, a jacket, and a cap called a kepi. These items of clothing were of butternut gray wool and were uncomfortably warm in June. The men were given socks, but no shoes or boots. Much to their disappointment, the junior reserves were given no rifles or other weapons. They were only allowed to use wooden swords in their initial parade-drill training session, which consumed the remainder of the afternoon.

Jim Henry and most of the others had grown up on farms and had been hunting with shotguns and rifles for years. They were less than impressed with the wooden swords. It did not help their morale to be told that afternoon on the parade field that the command "present arms" meant to hold the sword or rifle out in front and that the sword was intended just to help them know what to do with the rifle they would be issued later. Their morale was further challenged by being marched around in the heat of the afternoon with heavy wool uniforms on their backs. Jim Henry thought what a waste it was to fill brand new uniforms with sweat the very first day.

Still tired from the long hike of the previous day, Jim Henry went to sleep right after supper. The next morning, he and the other new junior reserves were given a good breakfast and were marched in a column to the Salisbury rail depot to catch the train to Camp Vance. When they got there, they were told that the train would not leave for some time and that anyone who wanted to could take a look at the Salisbury Prison.

Jim Henry and many of the other young enlistees decided to go and see the prison, which was situated on a sixteen-acre tract along the railroad track, very close to the depot. They went to the Bank Street entrance and asked the guards if they could see the prison. The guards allowed them through the gate in the high board fence surrounding the prison grounds. To their right, was a large three-story former textile mill. Six brick houses and a larger superintendent's house were arranged around the perimeter of a large square yard. There were several lesser buildings and lots of tents pitched under the oak trees that shaded the square. Hundreds of prisoners walked around or sat in groups around the square, and Jim Henry imagined hundreds more resting in tents or inside the buildings.

The guards told the junior recruits that the prisoner population exceeded the capacity of 2,500 and was rising fast because of a breakdown in prisoner exchanges.

———◆———

On Friday, June 25, 1864, 130 officers and men who were later listed in Confederate Army records as Company H of the

Seventy-Fourth Regiment of Junior Reserves, climbed with their gear onto a three-car train pulled by a brave little engine with a tall smokestack and loaded with wood and water. The train was quite crowded with people, baggage, and freight, in addition to the company of soldiers, who had to take turns standing up and sitting down. Yet it was better than marching the eighty miles to Morganton.

9

Junior Recruit

Shortly after their arrival at Camp Vance that same afternoon, Major McLean called the junior reserves into formation and told them that beginning the next week they would have one session of drill practice and one session of guard duty every day. He then dismissed them so that they could have the weekend to situate themselves in their cabins, visit the commissary, or go into Morganton to buy anything they needed. He told them that on Monday his staff would organize them and issue their rifles.

The cabins for enlisted men were doorless, unchinked log structures with four to six simple wood and cloth cots. Those with six cots had no standing room. The only storage space was under the cots or along the inside of the log walls where the men could hang gear and clothing from nails. After a while, a bugler blew retreat, a drummer boy who looked too young to serve rolled his drum, and the other young soldiers lined up and saluted as the stars and bars were lowered. They then assembled in the mess hall and went through the chow line, where they were served soup, a few vegetables, and a tiny amount of meat. Jim Henry learned from those who had arrived previously that food at the camp was skimpy.

After supper, the men congregated in small groups around the camp, talked and listened to a musician in their midst who strummed a banjo, joined by another who pulled a harmonica out of his pocket. Occasionally, they broke out into song, hymns,

Stephen Foster's melancholy songs, and marches such as "The Bonnie Blue Flag." One tune, "The Girl I Left Behind Me," made Jim Henry's heart ache. In spite of the peppy Irish melody, tears came to his eyes in response to the words:

Her golden hair in ringlets fair,
her eyes like diamonds shining.
Her slender waist, her heavenly face,
that leaves my heart still pining…
The vows we made to heav'n above
Shall ever cheer and bind me.
In constancy to her I love, the girl I left behind me.

——◆——

There was no organized activity on Saturday or Sunday, except for a poorly attended devotional service after Sunday breakfast in the mess hall. It seemed to Jim Henry that there was very little religious commitment among the men. In fact, it seemed that there was very little commitment to anything, not even to the Confederate cause.

Jim Henry used his free time to read his Bible, wash his clothes, and visit the commissary, where he bought some beef jerky and a few hard biscuits to go with it. He ate a little and saved the rest in his knapsack. He was disappointed in the slow and seemingly lackadaisical pace of camp life and looked forward to Monday, when the junior reserves were to be organized and armed with rifles. He could not understand why the newly arrived soldiers, who comprised a majority of the men at the camp, were not issued rifles immediately. What if they needed to be called into action?

When Monday came, Jim Henry was further disappointed to learn that the camp commandant, Major McLean, had left camp for unknown reasons and had left Lieutenant Bullock in charge of the camp with instructions to organize and arm the 277 junior reserve officers and enlisted men.

It was not until mid-morning that Lieutenant Bullock called the men into formation and organized them into three companies of three platoons each. There were not enough officers to serve as platoon leaders and some of the platoons had to choose their own leader. A long dinner break was scheduled in the middle of the day for that purpose. Then quarters were assigned to each unit, which meant that men had to move their belongings from one cabin to another. It was late in the day before the organizing was completed, and Lieutenant Bullock decided to delay the issuance of rifles until the following day.

10

Fall of Camp Vance

On the morning of June 28, 1864, Jim Henry woke, startled. It was still dark, but he was used to waking before dawn. It was a noise that roused him, an abrupt noise to which he was not yet accustomed. Then he knew. It was the bugler blowing reveille, not his dad's voice, to call the reserves to the center of camp to start their day. And instead of Jim and his brothers stirring and grumbling around him, it was his fellow junior reserves. He got out of his bunk and dressed. Instead of morning chores before breakfast, he and his compatriots had to line up for inspection.

The continued blowing of the bugle drew the reserves to the flagpole in the center of the camp. Lieutenant Bullock stamped his feet and yelled orders until he was satisfied with their formation. They came to attention as the Confederate flag was raised for the day. As the flag was raised, there was a second blowing of reveille just outside Camp Vance's gates. Sensing that something was wrong, Jim Henry and the men around him looked in the direction of the sound of the second bugle call. Lieutenant Bullock ordered the men to be at ease and strode toward the gates.

They heard the sounds of mounted men approaching the gates of the camp. As the gates blew open, a troop of Union soldiers in blue uniforms and armed with rifles raced in. The few sentries on duty made no effort to challenge them. They reigned in their mounts and stationed themselves inside the yard.

A man emerged from the group. He had enough braid on his

coat and hat to let Jim Henry and everyone else know he was in charge. Jim Henry's practical mind told him that armed resistance by the Confederates would be futile and their only viable options were to surrender or to try to escape. He also realized that they were at a numbers disadvantage and had practically no weapons.

As Jim Henry considered the possibility of escape, the Union officer in charge turned in his saddle and spoke inaudibly to his troops. Then he addressed the Confederates. "I am Captain George Kirk. I command the Third North Carolina Volunteer Infantry of the United States Army." He half stood in his stirrups. "We will strike the colors of the rebellion and raise the flag."

Kirk was an ordinary-looking man. He was young, but surely older than Jim Henry. His brunet beard was long and unkempt, but his high cheeks were clean and his blue eyes were like daggers that struck fear in Jim Henry.

"All of those who wear gray caps must now know that this camp is being seized." Kirk settled back into his saddle. "In order for this capture to remain bloodless, we expect for you all to obey my every order, and the orders given by any Union soldier who should speak to you."

He paused and looked around, then continued, "If you should try to escape, or fail to follow our orders, then we will have no mercy."

"I now speak directly to the officers of this camp." He pointed at Bullock. "You and your superiors will meet me in the tent to my left in three minutes to discuss the conditions of your surrender." He dismounted, handed off his horse, and walked toward the tent.

Lieutenant Bullock, who had slumped into the rows of his reserves, stepped forward and followed Kirk. Major McLean appeared from somewhere and joined him in a slow walk that made Jim Henry think of them as condemned men.

Jim Henry thought about this seizure of the camp he had barely lived in. He felt cheated and unsure of what would become of him now that he was a Union prisoner. He thought about the terms of surrender that Kirk would order. The men Kirk led were Southerners who chose to fight for the Union rather than the Confederacy. He wondered if there was a chance that he and the other junior recruits would be allowed to become federal soldiers to avoid imprisonment.

—◦◆◦—

While Kirk and the officers met, Union soldiers questioned the Confederates and wrote down their names and home counties. Jim Henry tried to speak to one of his comrades but was shouted down. "Prisoners may not speak unless spoken to." The order came with a shove in the back.

Jim Henry peered over the paper in which a man wrote down his name and saw that his last name was misspelled; instead of "Shore" his surname was recorded as "Share." He tried to point out the error, but the Union soldier scowled at him and moved on.

Jim Henry tried to count the Union soldiers. It seemed to him that there were close to two hundred men, all of whom were well armed. He said a quick prayer for the Lord's guidance in improving his chances of reuniting with Julia.

He knew that his chances of seeing Julia were not favorable if he were sent to a federal prison camp. Despite Kirk's threat that attempts to escape would be treated without mercy, he whispered to a few of colleagues, "Let's make a run for the woods behind us." He took off running, followed by Captain Sid Conrad and several enlisted men.

The front edge of the woods offered dense cover, but the cover thinned out as they progressed into the woods. Captain Conrad was not able to keep up with the other Confederate soldiers, and he ordered them to go ahead without him. Jim Henry and a few of the other Confederates covered him with brush in order to conceal him before they continued in their flight.

In a few short minutes, Jim Henry and the rest of his colleagues were recaptured at gunpoint, tied with ropes, and forced back into the camp with the other prisoners.

"Keep them apart from the others," Kirk ordered his men. "We'll make use of them." Jim Henry thanked the Lord that the escape attempt did not result in bloodshed, but he feared that Kirk would yet deal out the harsh punishment he had promised.

Captain Kirk then ordered the captives to surrender their belongings and to be prepared to move out of the camp upon an hour's notice. Jim Henry did as he and the other prisoners were told and prepared for departure. "Where do you reckon they'll take us?" the boy nearest him whispered. Jim Henry did not speak, but he was sure he knew. Kirk came from Tennessee and that was likely their destination. It sounded a long way off.

11

Captive

$\mathcal{A}$s Captain Kirk formed the column to depart Camp Vance, Jim Henry saw that practically all the prisoners were junior reserves like himself and that there were hardly any officers among the prisoners. Jim Henry heard the whispered suspicions around him that they had been abandoned by their superiors, but he wondered if it mattered. They were captives.

The prisoners were on foot in a column between their mounted guards. Other Union soldiers, unencumbered by prisoners, formed a scouting party in front and a rear guard behind.

Jim Henry had a six-foot rope tied around his neck and to the pommel of a soldier's saddle, like a dog on a lead. Johnny Knowles, the drummer boy, was tied to the same saddle. Jim Henry figured Johnny was a volunteer since he appeared to be no more than fifteen years old, certainly well below the conscription age of seventeen. The other prisoners were similarly tied, two to a soldier, and kept in the middle of the column, apart from the front or rear guard.

Although Jim Henry did not know the name of the soldier to whose saddle he was tied, he quickly learned that the horse's name was John. John had a habit of walking slightly more slowly than the horse ahead of him until there was gap of thirty yards or so and then he would trot to catch up. When he trotted, Jim Henry and Johnny Knowles had to break out into a run to keep from being choked and dragged by their necks. Jim Henry tried to lead the horse by holding the bridle, but the cavalryman, who seemed to be amused by the boys' predicament, ordered him to turn the horse loose. "This horse doesn't take orders from a Sesh."

"I am not a Sesh," Jim Henry said. "I opposed secession until the United States sent armed soldiers into the South. It was the Union army that lead most Southerners to support the idea of secession."

The soldier tightened up on the rope and raised his hand as if to hit Jim Henry, but must have decided the threat was enough. He laughed and turned away.

Jim Henry began talking to John incessantly. John responded to the encouragement and kept up with the pace of the other horses, so Jim Henry and Johnny weren't jerked around.

As the procession headed toward the northwest, some of the cavalrymen occasionally broke away from the column to raid farmhouses. The raiders returned with whatever booty they could find, whether cash, jewelry, horses, mules, or slaves, of whom Jim Henry counted thirty by the end of the day. Sometimes, Jim Henry heard gunshots ring out as the soldiers or their robbery victims fired at each other.

The one thing the raiders failed to steal was food. A three-man detail sent to steal livestock for meat failed miserably. As they approached a herd of cattle, the irate owner fired upon the soldiers and killed one of them. The other two returned empty-handed just as the column approached the Catawba River, which separated the inhabited area around Morganton from the mountains to the northwest. Although the population and the chances of finding food north of the river were minimal at best, Captain Kirk considered the danger of lingering on the south side of the river to be too great and ordered the men across.

The Catawba was some thirty yards wide and deep enough to require the cavalrymen to dismount so their horses could swim. As the prisoners were untied from the horses, some of them sensed their chance for freedom and submerged, allowing the current to take them downstream. Almost fifty of them escaped, although a few paid with their lives as soldiers fired round after round as the men came up for air. Jim Henry considered attempting to escape down the river. He had learned to swim in the Dobbins family's millpond, but not with his hands tied behind him. He was concerned that the current would not take him far enough fast enough. As much as he wanted to be able to go back and see Julia right away, he was not willing to jeopardize the chance of ever seeing her at all in this life.

As they marched to the northwest, the terrain became more rugged and houses almost non-existent. Just before dark, Captain Kirk ordered a halt at what appeared in the dim light to be a large meadow watered by a stream. The raiders set up a defensive perimeter and moved the prisoners, still tied, to the center. The horses were allowed to graze about the pasture. Because of their keen senses and their mannerisms when disturbed, the horses served as extra eyes and ears for those on sentry duty.

Jim Henry was so weary, he hardly had the energy to work with a fellow soldier to help each other drink from their canteens and to pull the bedrolls off their packs. As their captors offered no food, Jim Henry thought about eating some of the jerky and hard biscuits he had brought. Because there were so few farms on the north side of the Catawba River, raids for food were not likely to be successful. He decided he might have a greater need for his supplies later. He spread his bedroll on the soft pasture and collapsed on it, his weariness exceeded only by his need to pray. He thanked the Lord that he was alive and prayed that he might remain so and see Julia again. He asked forgiveness for all the things he had done that were not pleasing to the Lord, especially the choices he had made that had contributed to his present condition. He fell asleep reciting the Twenty-Third Psalm and thinking of the way he had been shepherded, the pasture he was lying in, and the streams where his canteen had been filled.

The next day, Wednesday, June 29, 1864, the raiders and their prisoners broke camp at dawn. Feeling hungry and knowing he would need energy for the day's journey, Jim Henry, put some of his jerky in a biscuit and wolfed it down while the column was preparing to move out. As they continued their march to the northwest the terrain became more rugged and the last semblances of farmland gave way to dense forests. Soon the column crossed a river. Again, Jim Henry thought of possible escape, but the guards were on heightened alert, and the river was not deep enough to risk an attempt.

Later that day, the land began to rise and Jim Henry saw that they had a steep climb ahead. He heard one of the soldiers ask another, "What is this place?" The answer was Brown Mountain. The word mountain made Jim Henry feel the distance from home.

Jim Henry followed the man in front of him, scrambling up a path scarcely visible in the dense woods, when he heard gunfire break out at the rear of the column. He and the men nearest him ducked behind trees, heads down.

"Keep moving," Captain Kirk yelled. "Stay in line and move double time. We'll make a stand from higher ground."

Kirk's troops drove the prisoners onward, with threats and blows when they didn't move fast enough. The pace was hard on the prisoners, who were on foot and had not been fed for two days. Those who did not keep the pace were cursed, prodded, struck, and even dragged by their necks. A few prisoners who were totally unable to continue were tied atop captured mules.

Eventually the gunfire died away. Captain Kirk called for a rest stop at last, beside a spring of good clear water.

Jim Henry drank deeply from his canteen and refilled it. Then he ate his remaining biscuits and jerky and stripped leaves from a sassafras tree to go with it. He figured he needed every ounce of energy he could summon in order to climb the mountain ahead.

He was afraid his captors might resort to shooting stragglers, and he had no intention of becoming one.

It seemed like their rest stop had hardly begun when Captain Kirk gave the order to move out. The weary men resumed their march, and in a very short while, Jim Henry could hear gunfire breaking out again toward the rear. It was clear to him now that the raiders were being pursued by Confederate forces, that rescue was possible. Captain Kirk immediately yelled to his men, "Halt! Set up defensive positions on both sides of the trail as you face downhill toward the gunfire."

He then sent a messenger to tell the rear guard to retreat back to the main column's defensive position. In the previous attack, Captain Kirk had kept the prisoners away from the action, but now he ordered, "Line up the seshies fifteen or twenty feet in front of your firing positions and shoot any prisoner who moves."

The prisoners would be human shields to discourage the Confederate forces from firing into the Union position.

The soldier guarding Jim Henry and Johnny Knowles unhitched their ropes from his saddle and used the loose ends to bind their wrists. Then he ordered them to stand twenty steps in front of his protected position and warned them that if either of them ran he would shoot both of them without warning. Jim Henry knew that the soldier's Spencer rifle was a six-shot repeater and figured the chances of escape were not good. He began to pray, "O Lord, do not let it end like this. If you want me to die, so be it, but please give me more time."

Images of Julia flashed through his mind, and as he thought of her, his will to survive overcame any thought of resigning himself to the situation. He twisted his body and held his bound wrists out at an angle where they could be seen and bowed his head a bit so that his gray Confederate cap would be clearly visible. Then he shouted, "Johnny, make sure the attackers know who you are and where you are! Stay as visible as possible and you should be alright."

Their captors had allowed Johnny to take his drum with him, and he began a steady drumbeat to further prevent Confederates from stumbling upon them and taking a quick shot before identifying them as prisoners.

Soon Jim Henry could hear movement and from behind him Union soldiers began firing. He heard bullets tear the air from both directions as they passed by his head. Suddenly he saw Johnny Knowles clutch his chest, fall across his drum, and lie still. If the drummer boy uttered a sound, it was not audible above the din of battle.

Captain Kirk shouted, "Look at the damned fools, they are shooting their own men!"

The skirmish was short, as the Confederate force withdrew and the shooting ended. The only additional casualty among the prisoners was R.C. Pearson, who was wounded in the knee. Jim Henry felt badly that he had not prayed for Johnny Knowles's life in addition to his own, and that he now had to leave the boy's body behind.

Once again, Kirk's raiders and their prisoners began to move. The trail switched back and forth up a steep slope. Near the top of the ridge, Captain Kirk called a halt. Just off the path, stood an old abandoned house with exterior siding made of bark-covered laths. Captain Kirk called it the "Bark House" and made it his headquarters.

"Gentlemen," Kirk announced, "we will camp here for the night. Set up a defensive position in case the Confederates try to follow us up the trail."

His men dug rifle pits for themselves and positioned prisoners in front of them, where they would form a human shield.

That night, Captain Kirk's men and prisoners, except for those on sentry or guard duty, slept in a perimeter with the prisoners not made part of the defense in the center. Again, there was nothing to eat, but Jim Henry thanked the Lord for his deliverance and for the fact that all he and the other prisoners had to do was sleep. Jim Henry prayed until he fell into a deep and peaceful sleep, not only from exhaustion, but also from the release from a deadly situation to relative security in the center of the Union force.

A violent thunderstorm broke across the top of the mountain, with lightning and thunder all around. Although it lit him up, it didn't bother Jim Henry. It only reminded him that the Lord was in charge. When the rain stopped, he wrung out his clothes and tried to go back to sleep. Jim Henry had thought the heavy uniforms were too hot for summer, but on this cool night, the wool, even damp, felt good enough for Jim Henry to doze until reveille.

Early the next morning, Kirk's pickets in front of his position began firing their rifles and came running back to the main defensive position. Jim Henry could hear men working their way up the trail below and said a quick prayer that rescue would come, that he would live and see Julia again. This time Jim Henry, himself, was not one of the prisoners ordered to stand in front, and he thanked the Lord for it.

Soon a brisk firefight broke out and the Union troops were able to inflict heavy casualties from their well-prepared positions as they fired into the narrow gap through which the Confederates were approaching. The Confederates finally realized they were fighting uphill against a substantial force in a strong defensive position fronted by captives. The firefight ended as quickly as it had begun, as the Confederates led by Colonel H.S. Brown suffered so many casualties that they broke off the attack before all their men even reached the scene of action.

There were also casualties on the Union side. Union losses included one killed, one mortally wounded, and five slightly wounded, including Captain Kirk, whose arm was broken by a rifle bullet. No casualties were reported among the prisoners.

Later that day, Thursday, June 30, the captors and prisoners continued their march toward Tennessee. The landscape was a rolling plateau with occasional subsistence farms with no visible animals or edible crops. All the men were hungry, captors and captives alike. The rugged terrain had taken its toll, particularly on the captives, who had no horses and no military boots. Disabled prisoners with bloody feet and those who fell sick were allowed to ride on the back of mules.

By noon, every available mule was fully loaded with two or three prisoners. A few prisoners gave out completely and couldn't or wouldn't ride any further. They were taken aside as the column passed by and were never seen again. Jim Henry never knew for sure what had happened to them but assumed the worst when he heard gunshots ring out at the rear of the column. Any doubt was later removed when a fellow prisoner told Jim Henry something he had seen.

"There was this one-armed man out in the middle of a field he was plowing with a plow he had equipped with a handle on one side and with an extension on the other side to allow him to push with his shoulder." He looked around to see if any Union officer was listening before he continued. "He was still wearing his Confederate jacket with one sleeve rolled and sewn up to keep it out of the way. Captain Kirk walked to the middle of the field, pulled out his pistol, and shot the man dead."

Jim Henry felt helpless and discouraged. If Kirk and his raiders would kill a one-armed man trying to provide for his family, who was safe?

By late morning, Jim Henry was weary and longing for a midday rest break when he heard a cheer go up from the men ahead. As he rounded a curve in the road, he saw several mounted soldiers dashing across a pasture toward a small herd of cattle. The soldiers circled behind them, drove them toward the road, shot and immediately skinned and butchered them. Meanwhile other soldiers converted the pasture's split-rail fence into bonfires and cut saplings from the woods for spits. Within an hour the meat went from the hoof to the cooking spits, then was passed to the soldiers and finally to the prisoners. Within another hour the men, captors and captives alike, filled their stomachs for the first time in three days and continued their march. Late in the day, they crossed the border into Tennessee and the threat of further combat subsided. Jim Henry was pleased to be able to camp that night in relative safety.

On the fourth day, Friday, July 1, the column came upon a flock of sheep, which the soldiers quickly slaughtered, butchered, and parceled out among soldiers and prisoners alike. For the rest of their march, Captain Kirk's men and their prisoners had sufficient food along the way to regain some of their strength. On July 6, the eighth and final day of the march, they reached their destination, a small town along the railroad leading northeast from Knoxville. The name of the town, according to a sign on the depot, was Strawberry Plain, Tennessee.

The soldiers led their prisoners to a rectangular wooden stockade near the train depot with guard towers at each corner and a single gate.

Inside, there was nothing but open space—no shelter of any kind. A Union soldier who appeared to be in charge of the facility stood in front of the prisoners, most of whom were quite hungry, and he began to make an announcement. "We realize that many of you are very hungry. Your arrival was unexpected, and we will need a day to prepare food for you. I am hereby ordering those who are carrying food with you to try and share it with your fellow prisoners." He paused before he continued, "We don't want them dying off before tomorrow."

Jim Henry opened his pack and shared what remained of his food with his fellow prisoners. All survived until the next day when food arrived by train.

Some of Captain Kirk's men had secured fresh food at the depot and gave the remainder of their now four-day-old mutton to the prisoners. Before long, most of the prisoners who ate it began suffering stomach pain, followed by vomiting and diarrhea. Each time a prisoner moved quickly to the latrine, the guards would amuse themselves with such calls as, "Oh, Johnny, you got the Tennessee high step," or "Here comes another one with the Tennessee high step."

Jim Henry had finished his allotment of mutton the previous day and had not accepted any from his captors after the march was over. He thanked the Lord for sparing him from the suffering that some of those around him were experiencing.

Jim Henry made his way to a Union guard and asked, "What is going to happen to us?"

"You prisoners are fortunate to be out of the war. Life in the Union Army is not easy, and there are never enough provisions for the men." He seemed almost friendly, at least willing to talk.

Craving a conversation, Jim Henry described his trip to Strawberry Plains. "It was very difficult to be forced to march fording waist-deep streams and sleeping in the open for eight days with no rations for the first three days and one supply of mutton to last for the remaining five days in the heat of summer."

The young guard replied, "I sincerely regret your hardships, and I assure you that things will be better for you in the near future."

"I would like to believe you," Jim Henry said. "But I have seen that war brings out the worst in people who have the upper hand."

The next day, Friday, July 8, the prisoners heard a train arrive at the depot. They were escorted under heavy guard to the train. Jim Henry saw a line of cattle cars, some of which were already full of prisoners. As Jim Henry was forced up a ramp into one of the cars, he saw that there was no clean surface upon which to sit or lie down. The floor was covered with straw and cattle manure. In a wasted gesture, their captors had put a bucket in the corner for human use. He stepped inside the car, which quickly filled up with so many men that they had to stand shoulder to shoulder. As soon as the doors were bolted and locked, the prisoners began to kick the manure and the dirty straw out between the bars of the cars. A shot rang out and a guard shouted in a loud voice that anyone who kicked shit off the train before it left the depot would be shot.

Finally, the cattle cars lurched and the prison train headed west out of the depot. The men resumed kicking manure and filthy straw out of the cattle cars. With about sixty men to a car, there was not enough room for the men to lie down. Jim Henry spent the night sitting down and leaning against a fellow prisoner, someone he'd never seen before Camp Vance, but for whom he felt a brotherhood.

The train stopped in Knoxville to pick up additional prisoners, and the already crowded cattle cars were further packed.

On the following day, Saturday, July 9, 1864, the train arrived at Nashville, where they were ushered into an open stockade which was their home until they could be identified and processed. The processing did not begin until Monday, July 11, and there were hundreds of prisoners ahead of those on Jim Henry's train.

Finally, on Wednesday, July 13, it was time for Jim Henry to be lined up and identified for Union prison record-keeping purposes. Jim Henry gave his name, which the interrogator mistakenly wrote down as "Share" instead of "Shore." Without noticing the error, Jim Henry moved on with the line of prisoners. Later, when the roll was called and Jim Henry heard the name "Share" he pointed out the error in his name, only to be told that prisoners could not change the names on the roll.

Jim Henry asked to speak to the officer in charge, but the interrogator refused to allow him to do so. Jim Henry continued to protest that he only wanted to correct a mistake. The interrogator responded, "Even if there were a mistake in the name, correcting it would not correct the mistake the South made when it started the war."

Jim Henry said, "I don't believe in slavery."

"Slavery is not the problem. That is a matter that could have worked out over time. The problem is that the South left the Union, dividing our nation in two. Once we get this nation back together, I am sure you will get your name back together. In the meantime, I cannot help you."

The next day, Thursday, July 14, Jim Henry was put back in a cattle car bound for an unknown destination. By this time, the other prisoners from Camp Vance had been separated, and he did not see any of them in his car.

They rode all night and the next morning arrived at a military prison in Louisville, Kentucky. Here the roll was again taken, and he was on the roll as James H. Share. Again, he protested, and someone placed an "x" above his last name, but the name "Share" persisted as his official name in the Union records.

The prisoners from the train were placed in a stockade, where they lived in the open for two more days. There were long lines of men waiting outside the latrines, especially in the daylight hours, but even at night. Each day more prisoners arrived. Jim Henry could see that the war must be going badly for the Confederacy and that prison overcrowding was a huge problem. There was hardly enough ground space for everyone to lie down.

On July 17, 1864, after eight days in which the crowding seemed to be reaching the bursting point, all the prisoners were assembled for a roll call and loaded into boxcars for shipment to an undisclosed location. The prisoners were not told where they were headed, but soon after the train left the prison, they could hear a steamboat whistle, which told them they were crossing the Ohio River and heading farther north. Jim Henry feared the worst.

12

Hell

On July 18, 1864, Jim Henry felt the train slow down, and from inside the boxcar, he could hear the sounds of a city. He heard commands being yelled from men to their horses and mules, the occasional ring of church bells, and the clop of horses' shod hooves on the paved streets. The train crawled around some curves and jerked to a stop. Armed prison guards opened the boxcar doors, unloaded the prisoners, and herded them into an area surrounded by a fifteen-foot board fence with sentry boxes every sixty feet along its top.

As soon as the new prisoners were inside the compound, Jim Henry heard the gate slam shut behind them and his spirits dropped to a new low.

"Where are we?" he asked a guard.

"Chicago. Camp Douglas. Now shut up."

The guards ordered the prisoners to line up and place their knapsacks and everything in their pockets on the ground in front of them. Guards went through each knapsack and took away anything they deemed to be contraband, including knives, liquor, and money. Jim Henry had heard from both guards and prisoners that Union guards were supposed to put any money they took from a prisoner into an account, which could be drawn upon at the sutler's shop on the post, but he saw men's money go into the guards' pockets and knew that it would never appear again. He had a small amount of Confederate money, which he had hidden in his sock

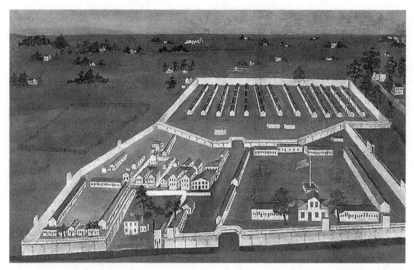

An 1864 painting by Albert E. Myers, a private in the Pennsylvania Volunteer Infantry. He painted this image while stationed at Camp Douglas in his studio of the tower of the Cottage Grove Hotel, opposite the entrance of the camp. Image courtesy of the Chicago History Museum.

before he left Camp Vance, and he took a chance by not pulling it out. It would be worthless to him while in prison, but he wanted to keep it in case there was still a Confederate government when he got out.

The guards seemed to take great pleasure in taking the contraband from the prisoners and barking orders at them. He had seen hostile attitudes and ill treatment on the part of some of Captain Kirk's men, and unsympathetic guards at Nashville and Louisville, but nothing like the hostility and hatred that seemed to consume the Camp Douglas guards. They shouted obscenities at prisoners for whom their most respectful appellation was "Sesh."

When prisoners did not move fast enough from the train to the compound, some of the guards threatened to shoot prisoners if they did not pick it up. To emphasize their point, they fired into the ground behind prisoners' heels. Then once inside the compound,

Prisoners at Camp Douglas. Source: Chicago Historical Society.

the prisoners were made to line up, and an officer of the guard paced in front of them and pointed to a white line of lime wash that ran around the perimeter, ten feet inside the fence. "This is what we call the deadline. One step over it and we kill you."

The officer went on to warn the prisoners that they were also subject to being immediately shot to death for talking or going outside the barracks at night or for gathering in groups to talk, even in daylight hours.

A guard near Jim Henry leaned close to him and said, "We enjoy the sport of hunting for prisoners who break the rules. I would take pleasure in catching you outside at night." Jim Henry tried not to flinch until the guard moved away. He looked around him and saw guards in the sentry boxes holding their rifles ready and fingering the triggers. He had no doubt that the threat would be carried out.

Then, several horse-drawn wagons with bodies of dead men stacked up like cordwood passed by them and headed out of the camp. While Jim Henry and the other new prisoners stood transfixed by the sight, none of the guards seemed to pay any attention.

Upon entering the camp, Jim Henry had almost gagged on a horrible odor. At first he thought it might come from the wagons of dead bodies, but the odor grew worse as the prisoners were marched further into the camp. The stench reminded him of the filthy cattle car, but more pungent. He was used to the smell of manure around the barnyard and with the smell of hog pens, but he didn't hear or see any animals, and this odor was fouler than any he had ever encountered.

As his column of prisoners was led through the camp, Jim Henry saw hundreds, maybe thousands, of men silently sitting or lying on the high ground of the compound, and near the lower end, he saw four rows of barracks. He counted sixteen in each row. The guards led them to the barracks area.

The buildings were elevated on four-foot posts. Behind the barracks, scores of men stood and squatted along the edge of a large ditch whose stagnant contents were overflowing its banks. An open sewer. The source of the stench. Beyond it was Lake Michigan, shining in the sun. It was summer, and the breeze coming off the lake caused the foul odor to permeate the camp.

The guards then divided the column of prisoners and assigned them to specific barracks. Jim Henry and about fifty other prisoners were assigned to one of the buildings that already was filled to normal capacity with over two hundred prisoners. The new prisoners were told to find a place to sleep and to sign a mess roll to be used in requisitioning food as men who bunked in the same area would eat together. There were twelve prisoners to a mess, which was the unit to which a set quantity was allowed. Then, stating the obvious, a guard said, "The latrine is out back."

Jim Henry would gladly have gone the rest of his life without relieving himself, but the very sight and smell of the latrine triggered his need. He had to step around many prisoners who sat or lay on the ground near the ditch, too sick and weary to move back and forth from the fetid ditch and who begged others to move them one way or the other. Some were only able to moan and groan. Some were unconscious.

One man, barely conscious, grabbed at Jim Henry's ankle and whispered, "If you love God, kill me. I can't take no more of this life."

The man was so filthy as he wallowed in his own waste that Jim Henry wanted to get away from him, but he paused. "Mister, I'll see if I can get you something to eat."

"I don't want food nor drink, nothing to prolong this life." The man fell back, resigned to his fate.

Jim Henry studied him a moment, then said a prayer for himself. "Lord, I know not what you have planned for me, but if it pleases you, give me strength to get out of here and return to Julia."

Fingers of standing water containing human waste and covered with algae extended from the open ditch into the barracks area. It was meant to drain into Lake Michigan, but the land was low and flat and it was obvious the channels could not handle the volume of human waste.

Jim Henry found a place where he could plant his feet on somewhat firm ground and get on with what he had to do. He forced himself to look down and saw no noticeable current in the ditch.

He instinctively looked around to see who could see him, and he saw a row of faces and torsos in the distance. People on the other side of prison fence, ordinary people so far as he could tell, certainly not prisoners or guards, looked over the wall at the sorry scene he was part of. They had to be standing on a raised platform to get a view. They were equipped with telescopes for viewing the prisoners.

For a moment, he looked to see if he could move behind one of the barracks so as to cut off their invasion of his privacy, but he realized he was not going to have privacy and went about his business. But the idea of those people on the outside staring at himself and his comrades as if they were no longer human caused something new to flare up inside him. Anger and disgust. And determination.

———◆———

Jim Henry set out to find a sleeping space on one of the platforms that lined the walls of the barracks and ran in rows down the middle. Men were lucky to get their body's length and width, plus a few inches so they could roll over. The guards had made it clear, all prisoners had to stay in the barracks from sunset to sunrise, with no candles. Jim Henry managed to find a niche for himself and burrowed in, feeling like one of a thousand earthworms dug for bait and stuffed into a tin can. He began to dread the first night.

The platforms were full, so Jim Henry and the other newcomers had to settle for sleeping space under the platforms, on the floor. Once he found his space, Jim Henry met the prisoner who had been elected captain of those who slept on one side of the barracks and signed the mess roll.

Most of the new prisoners, including Jim Henry, had not been fed for several days and were getting weak. It seemed to take forever for everyone to sign the roll and for the barracks captain to take his detail to the commissary and return with a large pot of mush. The men had been offered water at the train depots along the way. Some had cups with them and some shared a common dipper. Jim Henry always used his own cup in hopes of not exposing himself to every disease suffered by his fellow prisoners.

This first meal at Camp Douglas consisted only of corn mush poured out like soup.

"This is all there is?" someone behind Jim Henry in the line called out.

"That's it, brother. That's all we've seen for months. Once a day.

You eat it all now, there's nothing else till this time tomorrow."

"A man can't live on this."

"Some can, some can't. Who do you think cares?"

Jim Henry took his mug of slop and hunkered down to sip at it. A prisoner who had the look of a man who'd seen and suffered much squatted beside him.

"We used to get some half-rotten fruit and vegetables, but nothing like that since Colonel Sweet took over in May. The scurvy's gotten bad since then."

Jim Henry looked around him at the faces of the old-timers. He knew the symptoms of scurvy and saw them in the hollowed-out faces and the mouths missing teeth. He'd heard from childhood that it was a terrible way to die.

Even that afternoon, in broad daylight, he'd glimpsed rats, mice, and roaches skulking in the grass and hiding under the barracks. When he tried to settle down for the night, he discovered that the vermin ran across the bodies of men trying to sleep.

Bedbugs and lice crept out of the straw into his clothing, hair, and crevasses of his body. Mosquitos sang in his ears. Yet somehow, men around him snored and cried out in their sleep. He guessed he'd get accustomed to the conditions and the stink, as they had, and tried to rest.

———◆———

On his second day in the compound, Jim Henry received his ration of food for the day. He took it outside the barrack. A prisoner who looked like he had been at Camp Douglas a long time began to approach him with his own ration of food. He quietly sat down next to Jim Henry as they ate. Jim Henry felt uneasy as he did not want to draw any attention to himself at risk of being shot by one of the guards. However, disregarding the possible consequences, the prisoner leaned in to introduce himself.

"Hi," he began quietly.

"Hello," Jim Henry said, trying to speak as little as possible.

"What's your name?"

"Jim Henry." He looked around, nervous. "Aren't we supposed to avoid talking? They told us we would be shot for doing so."

"They usually don't mind two people talking in the daytime. They are more cruel after dark. Did you hear the shots last night?"

"I did. Do you know what happened?" Jim Henry asked the prisoner.

"A man began to feel ill and when he got up to ask permission to go outside, he was shot to death before he could even get a word out."

Jim Henry could plainly see that the guards cared not one whit for the life of a prisoner and that the guards were not at all worried about disciplinary action being taken against them for killing prisoners.

After he had eaten, Jim Henry watched as a new trainload of prisoners was released into the compound. He saw them gather in front of one of the guards just as he had done the day before. One of the newcomers, who had not even heard the rules yet, stepped across the deadline and was immediately shot to death.

The rest of the new prisoners were processed as though nothing had happened. Jim Henry redoubled his resolve to obey the prison rules.

He learned that the no-talking rule was flexible, sometimes enforced, sometimes ignored. New prisoners did not even have a chance to settle in their barracks when they were pressed on every side by veteran prisoners who wanted to know the latest war news. The long-time prisoners, known as "pickled sardines" or "salt fish," were dismayed to learn that Tennessee had been lost and that raiders had even been able to capture a Confederate military facility such as Camp Vance. They were further dismayed to see that the Confederacy was conscripting seventeen-year-olds who were now being captured in large numbers.

Jim Henry was amazed at how little the prisoners knew of what was happening in the outside world. It was then that he learned prisoners were not allowed to send or receive mail. His heart sank as he felt the separation from Julia becoming wider than it had ever been. He wondered how Julia was getting along and how she would react to not hearing from him for a very long time. He prayed once more for strength to endure prison life and to see her again.

———◆———

In looking for a place to sleep, Jim Henry had asked a man who occupied a space on the floor whether he could use the apparently empty area next to him. The man was agreeable. Then Jim Henry noticed that he was obviously sick. Looking around he saw that many of those on the floor and on the platforms that day were suffering from disease or malnutrition. Once he'd seen the food they were given, Jim Henry understood why they were wasting away. Some of the sick men were so hot and sweaty that Jim Henry figured they had typhoid fever or some other infectious disease. He learned that some had died from diphtheria as a result of being given contaminated milk, and that problem had supposedly been solved by eliminating milk from the diet.

The weak and feverish condition of many of his fellow prisoners seemed identical to the condition of his two younger sisters just before their deaths. He remembered the grief and mourning of his loving parents, then thought of the man who had begged to be killed rather than stay in this place. He knew that many of the prisoners would not be there for very long, and understood that they might welcome death. But he renewed his resolve and thought he must harden his heart against others' suffering, something his mother would never have advised him to do.

———◆———

A man with obvious smallpox sores lay near Jim Henry's bed space. He raised himself up and said to the newcomers, "You fellows be sure to inoculate yourselves with smallpox pus before it is too late. If you wait too long, you will become too weak from staying here to survive the inoculation. I may or may not make it, but I can help you survive."

"How do you do it?" one of the men asked.

"You take some of this pus, find something sharp to scrape a hole in your skin, and rub it in. You'll get smallpox, but not as bad as you would if you caught the disease the normal way. With inoculation you get sores quicker, but you are likely to get over it sooner. If you survive, you will be immune from then on. But don't get the pus from me. Get it from someone who has only a mild case, and you'll increase your chances of surviving."

The idea of inoculation was too much for Jim Henry to contemplate right then. He eased out of the barrack, hoping he could find a healthier place to sleep. Several other newcomers joined him.

For the next several hours, Jim Henry and other new prisoners went through barracks, one after the other, in search of safer accommodations and found none. The barracks were full of malnourished and sick men, many of whom seemed to be barely hanging on to life.

It began to rain and the ditch that served as a latrine overflowed more than before. Jim Henry and the other new prisoners had to pick their way around ponds of putrid water, brownish with a greenish algae overlay, and up to several inches deep. The more he saw, the more depressed he became about the prospects of his survival in Camp Douglas.

He finally decided to run back to the first of the barracks he had visited, where the smallpox victim had offered advice on inoculation as a way to survive.

Jim Henry went back to the man who had the sleeping spot on the floor next to his. They called each other bunk mates, although there was no bunk, only a few square feet of floor space in the midst of a long line of other prisoners who shared the floor. Four feet above them was another long line of prisoners wedged on the platform.

"What do you think of this inoculation idea?" Jim Henry asked.

"I did it when I first got here. I got a little sick but came through it. I've seen for myself, some die from the inoculation but most live and never get the full-blown small pox."

Jim Henry found a man who had just been released from the camp's hospital, known as the pest house, with a mild case of smallpox who was willing to donate pus from his sores. Jim Henry scraped through his skin on his arm with a needle and applied a generous dose of pus from the victim's sores and tied his handkerchief around his arm to keep the pus from being brushed away. He went back to the bunk he shared, knelt down, and thanked the Lord for his health and for guiding him to have the inoculation. He prayed that he would survive, but that if he did not, that the Lord would take care of Julia and let her know how much he loved her. He then left it in God's hands with the Lord's prayer and its phrase "thy will be done." Jim Henry felt at peace about it and was confident the decision to be inoculated was the right one.

——◆——

It was only a matter of days before Jim Henry developed a fever and small red sores began to appear all over his body. Jim Henry's bunk mate suggested that Jim Henry seek admission to the pest house, where the sickest and most contagious prisoners were held to isolate their infections from the rest of the prison population.

Jim Henry went to the pest house, which stood next to the camp's hospital, and requested admission. He was escorted under guard to the admission room, where he had to line up with other prisoners, many of whom could hardly stand. To Jim Henry, it appeared that most of the others were clearly worse off than he, and he hoped there would be room for him. The most pitiful of the sick prisoners were the scurvy victims, with gums and lips rotting and teeth falling out. He could see their faces disfigured with pain and what appeared to be rotting and dead flesh. Some prisoners were covered with festering smallpox pustules with flies either buzzing about them or covering their skin, depending on whether the victims still had enough strength to chase them away. There was constant noise from those moaning and coughing. Some coughed so deeply their whole bodies shook. Some were so weak they could hardly cough. Some of the prisoners unable to stand in line lay still and quiet on the floor. Jim Henry prayed that their silence meant sleep and not death.

For many there was no hope. Jim Henry had seen prisoners carrying their dead comrades from the pest house to the dead house at all times of day, but especially in the early morning, when the bodies of all who had passed away during the previous night were collected. He wondered where and how those who died were laid to rest, if their loved ones would ever know.

Jim Henry considered measles to be the least dangerous of the diseases he saw in the pest house, yet his mind kept going back to Lewis Williams, Julia's brother, and the fact that he had died of measles in a Confederate hospital in Wilmington, where conditions must have been much better than at Camp Douglas. He asked one of the doctors about it and was told that measles might not be as deadly as some other diseases, but that it weakened the body so that it became susceptible to pneumonia, which was very deadly. Jim Henry then turned the conversation to his own case.

"Can the same thing happen with smallpox?"

"Sure can."

"Do you think I am likely to die?"

"Smallpox is a deadly disease, but you look pretty strong to me and the fact that you inoculated yourself with it rather than catching it naturally means you have a better chance of living. They taught us here at the medical school that smallpox inoculation was practiced in Europe as early as the 1500s and it was known in other parts of the world. An Indian recommended it to Cotton Mather, so the Massachusetts Bay Colony avoided a major outbreak. Inoculation was used by the Continental Army. At first, George Washington refused to have his men inoculated because of the risk, but when they got to Valley Forge and Washington saw how his men were going to be cooped up in close quarters all winter, he changed his mind and ordered his men to be inoculated."

Jim Henry had seen that smallpox was rampant in the close quarters of Camp Douglas, and he was grateful to the doctor for letting him know his decision was the same as the one Washington made for his men.

Then he asked, "Is it true that you doctors are here as volunteers?"

"Yes," came the answer, "we are all volunteers. The prisons are being run with what is called 'all due economy' and that doesn't allow funding of physicians for prisoners. I am on the medical faculty at the University of Chicago, just as most of the other physicians are. We come here as often as we can for the same reason Jesus healed people—to make them well and also to let them know God. The university started as a Baptist school to train ministers of the gospel, and that is our heritage. Are you a believer?"

"Yes," Jim Henry said, "and I thank God for you."

Jim Henry was amazed that physicians would come as volunteers at no small risk to themselves to try to save prisoners from infectious diseases while the U.S. government, which was in charge of the prison, did little to avoid or alleviate the problem. He worried about contracting scurvy and was glad to see that patients in the hospital and even in the pest house were given fruit and vegetables as a regular part of their diet. Jim Henry surmised that the idea was originated with the University of Chicago and its volunteers, and not with the authorities in Washington, D.C.

As his fever mounted and his sores multiplied, Jim Henry was concerned about the risk he had taken and wished he could talk with Julia about it. Ever since the time of his capture, he had wanted to write Julia to let her know that he was alive, but there was no opportunity during the forced march and train journey.

Occasionally prisoners would try to get messages to the outside world by putting them on kites that they would release over the fence. The necessary newspaper, glue, sticks, and string were sometimes obtainable from a guard who needed some extra spending money. Sometimes kites had to be improvised by mixing flour or bread and water for glue and stripping clothing or bedding for string. Jim Henry considered trying to send a kite message to let her know that he was alive, but knew it would be impossible for Julia to reply and that the risk was too great, that the kite might fall into the wrong hands, and that the authorities might trace the kite message back to him.

Besides, he knew she would not give up on his returning after the war—no more than he would give up on seeing her again.

In spite of his own sickness and the misery about him, Jim Henry appreciated the pest house because he had his own cot and an improved diet. After a week, his fever began to break, and although quite ill with festering sores, he was sent back to his barrack in order to free up space for worse cases.

Upon arrival in the barracks, Jim Henry found he had lost his sleeping space. He had been displaced by an incoming prisoner. Jim Henry felt an urge to go and thank the man with the advice to inoculate against smallpox. When he arrived at the man's sleeping place, he found it empty as the man had just died. While he was dismayed at the man's death, Henry was pleased to have his space, as it was on the raised platform instead of the floor.

After several days, Jim Henry's sores began to dry and he began to feel better. He thanked the Lord for his deliverance from the disease. He only wished that there was room in the pest house for all the men who were sick. He also wished there were inoculations for the other diseases that were constantly claiming the lives of prisoners. He felt fortunate, indeed, to have recovered. In spite of his grim surroundings, Jim Henry felt a joy that the Lord had spared him, and he repeatedly thanked the Lord for preserving his life and restoring his health.

Jim Henry felt the loss of the smallpox victim who had died, as he was the only person at the prison with whom he had had a significant conversation. Most of the prisoners had no interest in establishing relations with others and tended not to show much interest in conversation of any kind. Jim Henry had learned through the grapevine of the danger of talking with a Union agent posing as a prisoner or with a prisoner who had become an informant on his fellow prisoners. Such persons were known to be operating in the prison in order to provide the guards with intelligence as to what was going on among the inmates.

Second, many of the prisoners were too weak from malnutrition and disease to show interest in others. Each was interested primarily in his own survival. Jim Henry soon saw that even those who seemed healthy were not very interested in human interaction. It seemed that each man tended to be so depressed with the hopelessness of his own situation he lost all interest in other people who were equally depressed and had nothing to offer in the way of support.

One of the exceptions was Harry Smith, one of his bunk mates on the raised platform. Harry had been in the prison so long he was known as a one of the pickled sardines. Jim Henry thought Harry could not possibly be a federal agent or an informant because surely the Union would not keep an agent or a cooperative informant in prison indefinitely.

The thought of escape crossed Jim Henry's mind as he felt better, and he thought it safe enough to discuss it with Harry. Harry told Jim Henry that there had been escapes by means of tunnels, which had originated beneath the barracks, but that the barracks had been elevated four feet off the ground with open space beneath them in order to preclude such tunneling. He said that one escape had been effected by climbing over the board fence, but the fence had been raised from fifteen feet to twenty feet in height and now climbing it was out of the question.

Jim Henry asked the sardine if there might be another way out. The sardine answered, "The guards tell me that before the prisoner exchanges ended in 1862, you used to be able to have a friend or relative buy your way out by paying $250 to a Mr. Orville Browning, a former congressman and friend of President Lincoln. He would regularly intercede with the president and later on directly with the head of the prison system. People cannot do that anymore, though, because with no mail in or out of the camp and with the refusal of the Yankees to disclose any information concerning the identity of prisoners, there is no hope of even letting your kin people know you are in prison, much less arranging with them to pay the $250 ransom money.

"It also used to be possible to get out by becoming a galvanized Yankee, by swearing allegiance to the Union and joining the Union Army."

Jim Henry said, "Well, there must be some way to escape. We can't just sit here. At the rate people are dying there would hardly be anyone left in another year were it not for the new prisoners being brought in by the thousands. At the rate they are bringing them in, a lot of people are going to have to die to make room for them. Who can I talk to, to explore the escape possibilities?"

Harry provided no suggestion.

The next day a guard accosted Jim Henry and asked him to follow him. The guard led him to a shack where a Union officer was seated behind a small desk. The officer had Jim Henry identify himself and then he said, "We know you have been talking about escaping."

Jim Henry stood silent.

"How would you like to ride the mule?"

Henry had not seen anyone ride the mule, but knew that it was an excruciating punishment in which a man was tied astride a sharpened board with weights on his feet and bounced around the camp until thoroughly tortured or even permanently incapacitated.

"I haven't done anything," Jim Henry said.

"The only way you can avoid a mule ride is to tell me the names of everyone you have talked with about escaping."

Jim Henry thought about his conversation with Harry and wondered whether Harry had tipped the guards off or whether someone else might have overheard them. He finally decided that if the officer knew he was involved in the conversation, he also knew that Harry was involved, so he said, "Harry Smith."

"Who else?"

"Nobody else."

"If you lie to me, it won't be just a mule ride. You'll hang by your thumbs. Now, who else?"

"Nobody else."

"What did you say to Harry Smith?"

"I just brought up the subject and asked his opinion."

"What did he say?"

"He said in so many words that it was not a good idea to try to escape."

"What else?"

"That is all there was to it. We were certainly not planning to do anything and still aren't."

"Better not mention the subject of escape to anyone again—ever!" The officer brought his fist down on the desk as if he'd like to smash Jim Henry's face instead.

"Yes sir."

"You are dismissed."

As he made his way back to the barracks, Jim Henry knew that he had had a narrow escape. The seriousness of it was thrust upon him soon enough. He watched a group of guards raise up a ten-foot-tall wooden frame, at the top of which was a hapless prisoner tied astride a two-by-four board with its upper edge sharpened. As if the prisoner was not suffering sufficiently, the guards tied heavy weights to his feet. They made great sport of bouncing the apparatus up and down and occasionally dropping it hard on the ground, and the victim screamed and groaned as blood soaked his trousers.

Several weeks later, Jim Henry heard a commotion in the prison yard, and when he went to investigate, he saw three prisoners hanging by their thumbs, tied to a board mounted just high enough so their toes could barely touch the ground. When they became too weak to support themselves, they hung by their thumbs, which quickly became dislocated, but still supported their full weight.

One man threw up from the pain and the others begged for relief. After what seemed an eternity, the dangling figures grew still and silent as they lapsed into shock. It was only after they became unconscious and insensitive to further pain that they were cut down and allowed to be carried back to their barracks by their fellow prisoners.

Then there was the dungeon, a room dug in the ground with a small trap door at the surface, through which the prisoners were dropped. The dungeon was located near the perimeter fence, and Jim Henry had heard that some men had dug out and escaped. The guards remedied the situation by crowding so many prisoners into the dungeon that they could hardly turn around or even breathe, much less dig a tunnel. There were no arrangements for handling human waste, which accumulated on the floor and fouled the inadequate air supply.

The principal offense for which people were put in the dungeon was for attempting escape. There had been a number of escapes early in the war, and the stories were handed down from salted sardines to newcomers. Yet on Tuesday, September 27, 1864 some half-dozen men made a partially successful escape attempt. One of them knocked a hole in the wooden fence with a heavy maul before guards shot out part of his jaw and tongue. Several were wounded, but some got away. Most were quickly recaptured and put in the dungeon.

Jim Henry had seen from his first day at Camp Douglas that some of the officers and guards had an eagerness to shoot at prisoners, even when they were not attempting to escape. All doubt was removed when he saw two prisoners walking along so engrossed in a conversation that they did not notice they had crossed the deadline and were approaching the perimeter fence. Without warning, several shots rang out from a guard shack atop the wall, and the men fell mortally wounded. For the guards, it was not cruelty, but sport. Sometimes they even said they were going to go "sporting," which meant going out and watching prisoners to see if they could find an excuse to shoot one. It didn't take much of an excuse. It could be a prisoner talking at night, going outside the barracks at night, or accidentally crossing the deadline.

From day to day and from night to night, continual gunfire reminded Jim Henry of the guards' propensity for sporting. It was said that a prisoner could hardly afford to snore at night for fear of a bullet coming through the wall.

One night, Jim Henry asked Harry how the guards could be so cruel. Harry said, "They do not look on prisoners as human beings. It is the way some people look at Negroes. And you ought to see how little regard they have for the life of a Negro prisoner. One who fought with the South was shot dead as he entered the camp. The guards feel that no Negro belongs in the Confederate army or in this prison."

From the tone of Harry's comments, it seemed to Jim Henry that Harry could not possibly be the man who informed on him, and he was tempted to push the conversation further, but the risk of saying something that would not sound good if reported to his captors was too great. Jim Henry could only say, "Thanks for letting me know how things are."

As the summer wore on, Jim Henry lost strength and his body began to shrink from the inadequate diet of corn mush. The problem was not just physical, but mental. He began to feel isolated and depressed even though he was crowded in with countless other prisoners who shared his fate. It seemed that it was every man for himself. There were quarrels over bunk space, food, and whether a person was so sick they should be excluded from the barracks. The only exceptions he could think of were the dying prisoner who had insisted that Jim Henry inoculate himself with smallpox and the Baptist doctor in the pest house who voluntarily risked his life to help those in prison. Now Jim Henry had access to neither, and he cut himself off from Harry. He felt alone in a prison where everybody cared only about himself and his own misery.

Jim Henry thought the only solution was to establish some human contact again. He suggested to the men in his mess that they share their food with those members who were suffering the most from malnutrition. Eight men agreed to participate. The most emaciated man in the mess previously had a tall and well-muscled body, but his large frame had been reduced to skin and bone by the prison rations, which allowed him no more food than anyone else. He declared that he could eat more food than was allowed for all eight of the men. The men called him on it by offering their food, and he ate the entire day's food ration of all eight.

Jim Henry felt so badly for the other men who missed their only meal for the day that he quit pushing the food-sharing idea, but thereafter he occasionally noticed prisoners giving some of their food to those suffering the most from malnutrition. He would long remember the incident as a measure of the small amount of food rationed out to prisoners. He could not help but think that the inadequate rations were known to high federal authorities.

From the day Jim Henry had first entered Camp Douglas, he saw the people on raised platforms outside the camp looking at the prisoners with telescopes and binoculars. They always seemed to be there. He asked other prisoners who the watchers were. He learned that the platforms were profit-making ventures whose owners charged admission for people to climb up and view the prisoners across the top of the fence. Camp Douglas was only four miles southeast of the center of Chicago, and there was a horse-drawn trolley service from there to the prison, to accommodate the curious. Interest in the war ran high in Lincoln's home state, and Chicago provided the most Union soldiers per capita of any Northern city.

Big crowds rotated through the viewing platforms when the weather was good, especially on Sundays and holidays. Some of the prisoners had shown their feelings about the viewing stands by turning their backs, dropping their drawers, and mooning the viewers.

As time went on, the prisoners became less annoyed by the observation towers and even began to see them as beneficial in allowing the outside world to see how bad prison conditions were. Surely there was someone out there who could see the injustice, the suffering, and the death taking place within the prison. Possibly, observers would be moved enough by what they saw to say something to authorities who could do something about it. Prisoners began to make a point of showing their tattered blankets and filthy worn out clothes where they could not be missed by those in the towers. They would also make a point of carrying the carcasses of the dead from the barracks to the dead house during the middle of the day whenever possible so that viewers could see what was happening.

In the late summer of 1864, Jim Henry began to see evidence that people in Chicago were becoming concerned about the plight of the prisoners. Jim Henry had already been impressed by the Baptist-sponsored University of Chicago hospital personnel who volunteered to help care for the seriously ill prisoners. Now he heard rumors of friction between the people of Chicago and Colonel Benjamin J. Sweet, who had taken over command of Camp Douglas in May 1864. By the time Jim Henry arrived, Colonel Sweet had already established his reputation as the most brutal commander the camp had ever had.

13

Release

*A*s the last few months of the war dragged on, Jim Henry wondered how soon it would be over and when he could go home. The guards told prisoners they would have to do time after the war was over. President Lincoln's assassination raised fears of retribution. Although General Lee surrendered in April 1865 and the war came to a formal close, it was not until June 6, 1865, that general orders were issued from the adjutant general's office in Washington, D.C., calling for the discharge of prisoners. On June 17, 1865, "James H. Shaw, Conscript-Unassigned" took the oath of allegiance to the United States and was released with a destination of High Point written on his papers.

Jim Henry and the other prisoners had been given a choice of swearing allegiance to the United States and getting government transportation toward their homes, or not so swearing and being left to find their own way. Jim Henry was not happy swearing allegiance at the behest of his enemies, but he figured he would eventually have to do it anyway. And he knew he was so weak he could have never walked all the way home. He wanted to see Julia at the first possible moment and needed to get home before his strength gave out.

The men were packed into freight cars and given small sacks of food to last them until they reached Philadelphia. Along with the rest of the former prisoners on the train, Jim Henry was directed to the Soldiers Home, where he had his first good meal in more than a year. From there the former prisoners were shipped by train to Wilmington, Delaware, and put on a steamboat bound for Virginia by way of the Chesapeake Bay. The war had resulted in the severance of rail connections between North and South.

Along the way, the steamboat stopped along the edge of the channel and rested at anchor for several hours. Word spread that the steamboat captain was drunk and the boat would not move until he sobered up. Someone shouted, "swim call," and most of the former prisoners seized the opportunity to strip down and jump into the Chesapeake Bay. It was a warm July day and the water felt good. Jim Henry scrubbed his head and beard as best he could in hopes of getting rid of the lice that had been his constant companions for the past year. He felt an overwhelming pleasure in being clean. Then he went back to the boat, got his clothes, washed them in the brackish water and hung them to dry on the boat's rail. He did not want his family or Julia to see him or even get wind of him in the filthy condition to which he had deteriorated during his imprisonment.

The next day, the ship reached City Point, on the western edge of the James River just south of Petersburg. Jim Henry saw a small freight train on a siding next to the steamboat dock. The train did not have enough box cars to accommodate all the returning prisoners, all of whom wanted to leave on the first available train. Consequently, after filling the cars, the prisoners continued to climb on the train and took places on the tops of all the boxcars. There was still not enough room, so the last men to board had to hang on the best way they could between and beneath the cars.

Jim Henry was glad to land a perch on top of a boxcar. He was so pleased to be moving toward Danville and Greensboro that he hardly noticed when it began to rain. He was soon soaked to the skin, and when night fell, he began to shiver in the wind. The men on top of the car laid down close together to preserve body heat. Just as he was beginning to wonder whether he could last all night, the train stopped at a station and those who had reached the closest point to their homes got off, allowing others to upgrade their positions. Those hanging on the sides or bottoms of cars would move to the roof, and men from the roof would fill any available space inside the cars.

By the time they reached Danville, all the men were inside. Jim Henry marveled at the luxury of the boxcar as compared with the filthy cattle car which had carried him to Camp Douglas. The shelter from the wind and the darkness afforded by the closed doors enabled him to sleep like a baby even after the sun had risen.

At five p.m., the train reached Greensboro in its southward journey. Jim Henry got off to walk the remaining fifty-three miles west to his home by way of Kernersville and Salem. He wished the Moravians had not resisted the Southern Railroad's efforts to run its main line south through Salem, but there was no use thinking about blaming anyone. There was no way to shorten the remaining distance other than hitting the road. Jim Henry passed a man limping toward the west and asked if he needed any help. He then recognized that the man was an emaciated version of Sam Speas, a friend from Yadkin County. Speas said his leg had been shot up, but that it was almost healed and he thought he could make it home. Jim Henry had no choice but to stick with his friend, even though it meant a slower pace. The rest of the west-bound travelers passed by them and soon moved on out of sight.

Jim Henry and Sam were hungry and stopped at every farmhouse along the road to ask for food, only to be told that the men ahead of them had eaten everything the family had to offer. They finally succeeded in soliciting a few scraps of food, ate a few green apples from orchards, and made the fifteen miles to Kernersville before nightfall. A kind villager allowed them some food and a bush under which to sleep. Jim Henry had either not been able to wash off all the lice or picked up some more on the train ride, and he could not ask to be taken into someone's home.

The next day Jim Henry and Sam walked and begged their way for the remaining fifteen miles to Salem. Their frail bodies, unused to exercise of any kind, were not holding up well under the thirty-mile journey they had covered in two days, and because of Sam's wounds their pace was slow.

Toward the end of the day, they reached Salem and made a beeline for the Salem Tavern, managed by Jack Shore's friend, Mr. Chapin. Because of Jim Henry's emaciated condition, Mr. Chapin did not recognize him at first. When he finally realized who the gaunt figure before him was, Mr. Chapin's voice quavered and his eyes moistened. He immediately seated Jim Henry and Sam at a dinner table.

"What can I give you to eat?"

Jim Henry said, "We have no money."

"What I can give you to eat?"

"Anything. We'll be glad to eat anything."

In almost no time Mr. Chapin passed them a bowl from which they served themselves generous helpings of beef and vegetable stew. With no money and plenty of lice, Jim Henry did not have the heart to ask for a bed in the tavern.

"Mr. Chapin, would it be all right for us to sleep in the barn?"

"That would be fine, seeing as how a crowd came in just before you and filled up every bed in the place. Otherwise I'd insist that you have a bed to sleep in. Come on in for breakfast when you wake up."

Jim Henry and Sam woke up early the next morning, and after a fine breakfast, compliments of Mr. Chapin, they walked the mile from Salem to Winston, looking around the hotel and the courthouse for someone who might be driving a wagon or buggy to Yadkin County.

They had no luck and set out on foot. They crossed the Yadkin at Glenn's Ferry, hiked through the bottomland and on up to the Glenwood mansion on the high ground just west of the river.

Jim Henry was amazed to see no slaves in the bottomland fields, which were full of weeds. Along the road in front of the Glenn home, they saw a table laden with food. As they paused to look it over, Tyre Glenn came out of the house to greet them and to let them know that the food was intended for returning soldiers such as themselves. When he recognized Jim Henry, Mr. Glenn said he would ordinarily like to drive them home, but that he was too short-handed to do so.

"All the slaves are gone. Emancipation has not gone smoothly," he said. "Former slaves wanted to be paid cash wages, but when Confederate money became worthless, nobody had cash with which to pay wages. In fact, nobody knows whether there will be a cash market for cotton and tobacco harvested this year. We had plenty of garden vegetables to feed the people over the summer until crops could be harvested, but they were not willing to wait to be paid a part of the harvest. I had no choice but to move them across the river in hopes they would find cash-paying jobs else-where. Now I am left with more food from the garden than we can use, and I'm glad you are here to help eat it."

Jim Henry had his heart set on stopping by Wade Williams's nearby farm to see Julia before going home. He and Sam thanked Mr. Glenn for his kindness and continued their hike.

Soon they reached the Williams home, and Jim Henry hurried ahead to knock on the door. No one answered. Jim Henry looked around anxiously and began to see that the place was completely deserted. No crops were in the fields, only weeds. The grass in the pastures was so tall that obviously it had not been grazed for months. Jim Henry's anticipation turned into despair. Crushed by the disappearance of a dream about to be realized, Jim Henry walked in stunned silence until he and Sam reached the place where Jim Henry would turn toward his grandparents' home place and Sam would continue on the road toward his home near East Bend.

"Thanks for sticking with me," Sam said. He first stuck out his hand and then hugged Jim Henry. "I don't know if I would have made it without you. I'll always be grateful to you. May God help you find Julia soon!"

Jim Henry thought of Julia as he walked the additional mile or two to the John Shore home place. He asked himself, "What could have happened? Where could she be? How is she?" He spent the rest of the walk praying that she was all right and that he would see her soon.

John and Susanna Shore had just finished supper when their dog began to bark, and through the window they saw a lone figure walking from the road toward the house. John went out on the front porch and exclaimed "Great God Almighty! It's Jim Henry!" Susanna rushed through the door. Jim Henry broke into a run, and the elderly couple moved toward him as fast as their unsteady feet would carry them to embrace their grandson. They wept and praised God for bringing Jim Henry home alive.

Most of John and Susanna's children lived on the large acreage John had assembled, and John began ringing the bell used to call men in from the fields or in case of emergency. Almost immediately, Jim Henry was surrounded by a large gathering of aunts, uncles, and cousins, all ecstatic that he had returned.

Jim Henry was so busy hugging people and answering questions that he was given no opening to ask about Julia. Soon he could stand it no longer, stood back, and in a loud voice told the crowd, "On the way here I stopped at the Wade Williams home near East Bend and found it deserted. What has happened to Julia? Where is she?"

A hush went over the crowd. John responded, "Things have been hard since early this spring when the Yankees came through here and stole all of Wade Williams's livestock. The Confederates would at least pay something when they requisitioned livestock, but not those Yankees. Then the war ended and the freed slaves insisted on being paid cash wages, which nobody could pay. With no farm labor, all that bottomland Wade Williams was cultivating went from a blessing to a burden. Even if you could find share-croppers and produce a crop, there would be no assurance of a market for it. Yet you have to pay the taxes on land that is not making any money. Nobody has any money. Almost all of Wade Williams's slaves left when they saw he was unable to pay cash wages, but he did not run them off. A few stayed and are trying to live on what they grow in their vegetable gardens, but they no longer work for Wade."

"Where did the family go?" asked Jim Henry.

"Wade moved his family to Deep Creek. With his slaves freed, Wade was no longer subject to being shunned by the Quakers over there. I expect the family is back on their old farm near you."

"But what about Julia? Is she all right?"

"I'm sure she is," John said, "except for worrying about you. Since you've been gone so long, many people think you are dead, but the last time I saw Julia, she told me she had faith that you were alive and would be coming back."

Jim Henry wished there were some way he could overcome his exhaustion, tear himself away from family, and be on his way to see Julia, even though it would have been the middle of the night when he got there.

Jim Henry had no desire to remind himself of his war experi-ences, but family members pressed him. He only told them about his travels from Yadkinville to Salisbury, to Morganton, to Straw-berry Plains, to Chicago and back to Yadkin County. For the next hours, he answered questions about what had happened to him during the year he had been gone. However, at this time of rejoic-ing he could not bring himself to disclose the worst moments, such as being used as a human shield in the skirmishes, seeing hopeless men lying about the open sewer at Camp Douglas, see-ing men tortured or jammed into the dungeon, and seeing them die by the thousands from malnourishment and disease. He did tell them how he inoculated himself with smallpox pus, how rats served as a dietary supplement. His weight loss was so obvious that he had to let them know of the malnutrition and sickness that caused it, but he changed the conversation by telling of the killing and eating of the guards' dog.

After much rejoicing and storytelling, John Shore asked his son Calvin, then twenty-one years old and recently home from war himself, if he would drive Jim Henry home the next morning. Then to Jim Henry he said, "Calvin will be using one of your mother's horses. The Yankees got ours, but not all of yours. They were pastured in a small creek bottom a good distance away from the home place, and the Yankees didn't find them. If it had not been for those horses, we would be pushing and pulling plows ourselves. We can thank the Lord that Calvin has that horse to drive you home."

When the crowd of kin people had departed, Jim Henry said he would sleep in the barn, but his grandmother Susanna would not hear of it. The bath water was soon on the stove and Jim Henry got into the round metal wash tub and luxuriated in his first warm bath since the Saturday night before his departure for military duty thirteen months earlier.

At dawn the next morning, Susanna served a breakfast of recently gathered eggs and fresh corn pone. She apologized for the lack of ham or bacon and explained that Yankee foraging parties had gotten all of the livestock.

Uncle Calvin came with the buggy and the last leg of the long journey home was under way. In two hours, they passed the Bond School House and Jim Henry's mind was flooded with memories of the shootout. He wondered out loud whether Jesse Dobbins and those who went north with him had made it across the line.

Calvin said, "Jesse made it north all right. He is famous around here. He served in the Union army, and so far as I know has not come home yet, but I wouldn't be surprised to see him show up any time. It will be interesting to see how well he is received. Some see him as a traitor."

Just ahead lay the Jack Shore farm. They followed the road past the barn and stopped in front of the house. Jim Henry leapt from the wagon and ran for the front porch shouting, "Mother, Dad, anybody home?"

His mother, Eunice, came running out the door screaming, "Jim Henry! Praise the Lord!"

As they hugged each other, he tried to lift his mother off the ground and twirl her around as he had often done before, but this time his emaciated body was not up to it. He barely got her off the ground before he had to put her back down. As she squeezed her son in a tight embrace she exclaimed, "Thank you, Lord, for answering our prayers for this boy's safe return."

By this time, Uncle Calvin had dismounted from the wagon, and she greeted him warmly. "It's almost noon and the boys will be coming in for dinner soon. Will you stay and eat with us?"

"No thank you, ma'am," said Calvin, "I can hardly wait to get home, and there will be plenty of dinner for us there."

Hardly had Calvin left, when Jim Henry's father and brothers came in for dinner and found themselves rejoicing over Jim Henry's return.

Jack said, "Now that my own who was lost is now found, I want to kill the fatted calf, but there is no calf, fatted or otherwise. Stoneman's raiders took care of that. Beans and corn pone will have to suffice!"

At the dinner table, Jim Henry recounted for the second time the events of the previous year. Again he left out the most horrid scenes, both to spare his family the knowledge of his suffering and to shorten the time before he could see Julia. With a smile, he told his father and brothers, "As much as I would like to go back into the fields with you this afternoon, I feel the need to call on Julia."

"We'll saddle you up a good horse," Jack said.

Jim Henry galloped his horse the short distance to the Williams farm. As he approached the house, he saw a figure come out on the porch. At first glance, he knew it was Julia, and he urged the horse into a faster gallop. She came running toward the road screaming, "Jim Henry, Jim Henry, Jim Henry!"

Jim Henry pulled the horse up short, slung his opposite leg across the horse's withers and hit the ground running to Julia. They hugged and kissed and held each other while Julia's family assembled around them. Then the family members began embracing Jim Henry and expressing their joy with shouts and laughter.

"Won't you come into the house?" Julia's mother, Annie, asked.

"Please come," added her father. "We all want to know what has happened with you since we last saw you. We never heard anything!"

Jim Henry noticed considerably more warmth on the part of Julia's parents than he had received previously. For the first time since his capture, Jim Henry felt good about having decided to take up the side of the Confederacy, the side for which Julia's brother, Lewis, had given his life.

As much as he wanted to be alone with Julia, Jim Henry knew that he was going to have to tell of his experiences for the third time. This time he shortened the explanation even further by deleting not only the worst horrors, but also anything that might tend to make people feel sorry for him. He did not want to make anyone pity him, but more importantly, he wanted to finish the family visit as soon as possible and be alone with Julia.

Mercifully, Wade announced, "It's time to get on with our afternoon chores, everybody except Julia. She deserves some time with Jim Henry."

Seizing the moment, Jim Henry looked at Julia and nodded toward the door. In a moment, they had crossed the front porch and walked through the gate into Annie's flower garden. Julia almost sang, "I love you, Jim Henry!"

His mind was transported to the moment years before when she had first spoken those words to him, and now as then he was at a loss for any words other than, "I love you, Julia!"

He took her in his arms, and as she came up on her toes he lifted her off the ground and kissed her as never before.

They then nestled side by side in a hammock and Julia said, "I knew you were alive the whole time. Something made me know it. It must have been the Lord. I never had a doubt. It gave me a good feeling to look at all those full moons and to know that you would be looking at them too."

Jim Henry said, "It gave me a good feeling to do the same thing. I knew you were all right, but I have to admit when I came to your home in Red Plains and found it deserted, I started to worry."

Julia responded, "I started to worry about you, too, when I learned Governor Vance had gotten some letters from prisoners that showed how terrible the conditions were."

He said, "I do not know how those prisoners got mail privileges. We had none. Besides, I did not think there was mail service between the North and the South. Those letters must have been smuggled out of prison and hand delivered to the governor."

They both agreed that all that really mattered was that the war was over, and they were finally together. Jim Henry had not planned to, but took this moment to ask, "Will you marry me?"

"You know I'll marry you!" Then she added, "My parents think that eighteen is very young, and we'll have to satisfy my dad that we can make our way in the world and provide for our children."

"Don't worry," he said, "I'm going to work real hard and before you know it, we can show him I can provide a good living."

"It would be the best time for you to talk to Dad when we can show him that."

As he rode back home, Jim Henry realized that surviving the

war was only an initial problem and that now he faced a formidable financial challenge. From what he had already observed since coming home, the prospects of profitable farming in Yadkin County were not what they were before he left. His father, Jack Shore, had received financial help from his father, John Shore, in purchasing a farm. Under the current conditions, he could not expect his father to help him in the same way. His best bet was to work with his father to make the farm productive enough to give Jim Henry a start.

For the next three years, from 1865 to 1868, Jim Henry, his brothers, and father worked six days a week to wring all the productivity they could out of the family farm, but lack of a full complement of livestock and terrible growing conditions left them with three poor crop years in a row. The work during those six days started before sunup and ended after sundown.

The only time Jim Henry had left to visit with Julia was Sunday, and every Sunday afternoon he would call on her, first at the nearby Williams farm home, and later at the home Wade Williams built in Boonville. Because social norms did not allow unmarried couples to spend much time alone together, Jim Henry and Julia would take Sunday afternoon walks. Their most intimate moments were devoted to sharing their hopes and dreams, and many warm hugs and kisses.

Jim Henry's only other sources of excitement in his life were early morning hunts for deer, turkeys, or small game, an occasional trip to Salem to sell whiskey, and now and then a confrontation between men or even between entire families who had taken different sides during the war. There was enduring resentment about the Bond School affair, which had resulted in the deaths of two local men on each side at the hand of other local men.

Jesse Dobbins was mustered out of the Union Army in July 1865 and returned to Yadkin County on August 7. Shortly thereafter he came by the Jack Shore farm for a visit. Jim Henry missed him because he was visiting Julia, but at supper that evening Jack related Jesse's story to him.

Jack said, "Upon Jesse's return to the county, the high sheriff spotted him, laid a hand on him, and told him to consider himself under arrest. Jesse pulled away quickly and said, 'What for?' and the sheriff said, 'For murder.'" With that, Jesse ran, jumped on his horse, and rode straight to the U.S. Army headquarters in Salisbury. The next thing you know, a column of soldiers came from Salisbury and surrounded the courthouse in Yadkinville. The commanding officer announced he would have the courthouse and all its contents burned unless all indictments and other criminal records related to charges against Jesse Dobbins and his cohorts at the Bond School were delivered to him immediately. The clerk of court surrendered all the records, which the commander then turned over to Jesse Dobbins, who gave them to the men involved or to their families."

"That is great," said Jim Henry. "It looks like the war is finally being put to an end."

"That may be, but the sheriff's attitude won't change. Many think Jesse shot Captain West, even though it was probably someone else inside the school who did it. It will take a long time for the hard feelings to die down."

14

Hard Times

$\mathcal{J}$im Henry's life at home after the war was like heaven as compared with his time in Camp Douglas, but like hell as compared with life before the war. The farm was in poor condition due to Jim Henry's absence and Jack's trips to Saltville, on which he would take his third son, Bill, age thirteen, to drive the second wagon. This way the second son, Aquilla, age fifteen, could stay and work on the farm. Jack had continued to make these trips until the fall of 1864.

During that October, 5,200 Union troops attacked the fortifications around Saltville without success. On December 20, 1864, a similar Union force won the Second Battle of Saltville, and Jack was finally out of the salt business.

With limited manpower available, the farm work suffered, and the family had to ration its food. The situation became even worse when Stoneman's men took all the livestock except for Eunice's hidden horses. Without hogs or cattle, the family had to subsist largely on vegetables and corn pone. Jack made and sold one run of liquor, but the market in Salem had dried up because few had any money. Jack had to take his whiskey all the way to Cheraw, South Carolina, where it could be shipped down river to the export market.

The cash proceeds of the sale were a blessing to the family in being able to restock the farm and to buy such necessities as salt and gunpowder. With livestock in short supply, hunting was a necessary source of meat. The bushels of Irish potatoes the family dug from the garden and stored in the crawlspace beneath the wooden floor of their log home became a staple in the first winter after the war ended. The crawlspace was accessible by a horizontal door. Part of it had been dug out a few feet deeper in order to provide a storage place for vegetables to be kept cool without freezing.

Jim Henry was eighteen years old when he came home, and he was ready to earn money to be in a position to support Julia and start a family. He was disappointed in the difficulty of eking out a living because of the economy and the state of the farm. He worked from dawn to dusk with his father and brothers six days per week, and no matter how hard they worked there was always more needing to be done.

At supper one evening, Jack told Eunice, "There are just not enough hours in the day to get it all done."

Eunice asked, "Would it help if I brought dinner out to you when you are working on the other side of the farm? That way you would not have to spend time going back and forth in the middle of the day?"

It was a noble gesture on Eunice's part, but the new arrangement for dinner in the fields took its toll by adding to the hours of labor in the fields. Without a midday break the men were totally exhausted at the end of the day. The usual bantering and laughter at the supper table was absent as Jack and his sons were too tired to talk or even to eat much before rolling into their rope beds for the night.

In spite of the family's hard work, the rains did not come at the right time, and their efforts to salvage a decent crop in 1865 came to naught. Jack and his boys continued to work through the winter of 1865-1866 clearing land and preparing the ground for the 1866 crop year.

Then the summer of 1866 was another drought year, and most

of the corn dried up in the fields before it matured. Only the corn in creek bottoms survived. The family suffered but was able to produce enough food by carrying water, bucket by bucket, from a creek to their large vegetable garden. In 1867, they built a stone dam across the creek some distance upstream and cut an overflow trench from the resulting pond so water could reach the garden by gravity flow. However, it was so dry that summer that precious little water entered the trench, much less reached the garden.

When 1867, the third poor crop year, drew to a close, Jim Henry asked Jack, "How long do you think it will take for things to turn around and for me to be able to afford a wife and family?"

Jack said, "Who can say? Three bad crop years in a row, no good market for cash crops or even liquor, no government except the occupying military officers, and no tax-supported schools—it all tells us not to expect too much too soon. I don't see how I can do much for you and still support the rest of the family."

"I am not asking you to do anything. I need to find a way out of this box we are in. I may need to go off on my own to try to get work. Are you all right with that?"

"Yes, son, you know I am."

Jim Henry had often heard the phrase, "Go West, young man," which had been coined by Indiana newspaperman John Soule in 1851 and then popularized by Horace Greeley, who quoted it in an 1865 editorial in the New York Tribune. It became the mantra of thousands who left the East Coast to seek their fortune in the West. Jim Henry had never considered doing it, but he had a desperate need to break out of the economic impasse that blocked his way to marrying Julia. Then, in 1868 Jim Henry's friend Nate Poindexter told him he was planning to go to California, based on favorable reports from John Hauser, a neighbor who had gone there from Yadkin County the year before. Hauser was farming in the San Jose area and expected to clear a thousand dollars the first year.

As soon as he heard the news, Jim Henry began thinking of doing the same thing. Based on Hauser's report, he figured within three years he could possibly earn three thousand dollars, which would be enough to buy some land, build a house, and marry Julia. He knew that if he stayed in Yadkin County, there would be a chance he could waste another three years and be no closer to his goal. He was desperate to do something to break out of the pattern he was seeing.

———◆———

Over the next few days he discussed the prospect of going west with Jack and then with Eunice and the rest of the family. By this time, Jim Henry's five younger brothers were old enough to provide Jack the farm labor he needed. Jack helped Eunice through her initial reservations, and everyone in the family encouraged Jim Henry, even if they were reluctant to have him go far away again.

The following Sunday, after church and the noon dinner with his family, Jim Henry got on his horse and rode to the Williams home in Boonville. Julia heard him approach at a gallop and met him in the yard. "Why were you in so much of a hurry?"

"Two reasons. First, I can't wait to kiss you." With that he caught her up in an embrace, lifted and twirled her around, and planted a long kiss on her mouth.

"Well, what was the other reason?"

"It has to do with us. You know I have tried to earn enough to be able to get us a place where we can live and raise children, and it is just not working out. Crop failures are not the only problem. Even if we have a good crop year, there is not much market for it. Nobody seems to have any money here or anywhere else in the South."

"What can you do about it?"

"You remember John Hauser going to California?"

"Yes."

"Well, Nate Poindexter tells me that John has found there is a good market for farm products, and that land is plentiful and growing conditions are favorable. John sent his family a photo of himself all dressed up in a suit and tie. Of course, he could have rented his outfit, but it seems he is doing very well. He is in the milling business and said that the farmers bringing wheat to the mill are making very good money. He even said that a thousand dollars per year is not too much for a sharecropper to be able to clear, and for a cash renter who rents the land and supplies all the labor, animals, equipment, and seed, the annual earnings would be even more. Nate says he is planning to go out there in December. I want to go to make some money for the sake of our life together, but only if you agree and will wait for me."

"You know I'll wait for you, no matter how long. How would you get there? How safe would you be?"

"There are three ways to go. One is by rail to the Mississippi and by stage coach and wagon train the rest of the way. Another way is to go by boat from the east coast to the west coast by going around the tip of South America. The third way would be to take a boat to Panama, cross the isthmus by rail, and take another boat to California. I'm inclined to go by boat in hopes that I can earn some money as a crew member. I won't need a horse, and by selling Coalie, I could raise enough money to get to New York, where I will look for a job on a boat going my way."

"How long would you be gone?" Her voice dropped low and she looked down. He knew she didn't want him to go, but that she would wait as long as she had to. They were not children any longer, not after the war, the losses they had endured, the suffering they had seen.

"I figure it would take me at least three years and not more than five to make enough to buy a farm back here where we could get started. I know you said you would wait no matter how long, but five years may also be asking too much. Is it fair of me to ask you to wait that long?"

"You know I will. I love you, and I will miss you more than you can imagine."

As he put his arms around her, Jim Henry whispered, "I'll miss you even more. I love you and I always will."

After a long embrace and many kisses, Jim Henry observed, "The separation will not be easy. I thought my life was over when you moved to Red Plains, and we were so far apart for those seven years. Then the year of separation during the war was even worse because I couldn't even tell you that I was alive. From what we've been through, it's clear our love is strong."

"As the idea sinks in, it sort of scares me." Her skin turned pale, and she turned her head away as if to keep him from seeing her anguish. Then she said, "Shall we go in and say something about it to my parents?"

"Let's do," he said.

Wade and Annie Williams listened to the two explain the decision to wait to get married, and for Jim Henry to go to California. Annie held her daughter's hand, and they both had tears in their eyes. Wade cleared his throat and gazed out the window a moment.

"I appreciate your courage, Jim Henry. We'll take care of Julia for you," Wade said. "How do you plan to get there?"

"I would like to go as a crewman on a ship. If I went by land, I would have to pay for provisions along the way. This way I would hope to be making money while I'm traveling."

Wade rubbed his whiskers and observed, "They tell me that the wind gets ferocious and the ocean can be dangerous where ships go around the tip of South America. If I were going, I would take a ship to Panama, and cross the isthmus by rail. It's safer and faster. For the same reasons, you might want to consider going on a schooner rather than one of the larger square-riggers. The schooner with fore and aft sails that can be controlled from the deck are much safer for the crew, and they tell me they are faster."

"Going through Panama is what I had in mind. A lot will depend on what is available when I get to New York."

———•◆•———

Within a few days, Jim Henry had raised $120 by selling Coalie, the horse he had broken to a saddle and trained to pull a buggy. He felt he was giving up an old friend who had taken him back and forth so many times to Red Plains and had taken him on those memorable rides with Julia.

His last ride on the horse was on the day before his departure, when he went to Boonville to deliver Coalie to the new owner on his way to his final visit with Julia. As he walked up to the house, she came out to greet him with a kiss. She had on her prettiest dress, and the soft skin of her face glowed. To Jim Henry, she appeared more beautiful than ever, but there was a touch of sadness about her, and her eyes were moist as though she had been crying.

After going inside to speak to her parents, they went out to the garden. It was a sunny but cool day in early December 1868, and the only flowers blooming in the garden were the pansies. Jim Henry hoped their love would continue to thrive through the coming months just as pansies continue to bloom, in spite of harsh winter weather conditions.

They walked in silence, arm in arm, until Jim Henry made the mistake of showing a note of sadness. "When I dropped my horse off with the new owner, it brought back memories of all those times you and I rode together."

Julia was reminded of being forced to give up her own horse to General Stoneman's troops, and tears came to her eyes. "I can't help it," she said. "I loved Beauty and especially the rides we had together. Why did it all have to end?"

After a long, quiet hug, Julia's sobbing subsided, and Jim Henry

 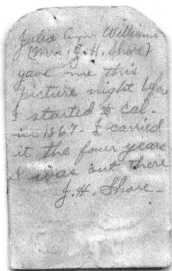

A print made from a daguerreotype of Julia Williams, who gave the picture to James (Jim) Henry Shore on December 15, 1867. Years later, he wrote on the back of the print, "Julia Ann Williams (Mrs. J.H. Shore) gave me this picture right before I started to Cal. in 1867. I carried it the four years I was out there."

responded, "It really doesn't have to end. That is what this is all about. We are just putting off being together for a time so we can have a good life."

"But three to five years seems like such a long time."

"Not as compared with a lifetime. We know that we have each other for always. Nobody can take our love away from us. If any two people in the world can make it through such a long separation, we can. There is no doubt in my mind about it."

"There's no doubt in my mind, either. I just want you to keep yourself safe. Look, I have something for you." Julia pulled from her pocket a small daguerreotype of herself encased in a silver frame.

"What a treasure. I'll look at you every day until I return." Their final kiss was long and passionate, and they both were breathing heavily as she whispered, "I love you more than you could possibly know," and he replied, "I love you even more." It took all their will power to pull away from each other.

As he walked home, Jim Henry paused to look at the photograph of Julia, and as he returned it to his pocket, he thought of how much he wished he could afford one of himself to give her. He hoped the $120 from the sale of Coalie would get him to California.

15

Seeking Passage

$\mathcal{E}$arly the next morning, Jim Henry and Nate loaded Jack's wagon with their bags and a barrel of whiskey, which Jack hoped to sell to Mr. Chapin at the Salem Tavern. By the time the sun was up, they were on their way to the train station in Winston. They went by way of Shallow Ford, as there had been such little rain that the Yadkin was quite fordable.

At the train station, Jim Henry and Nate purchased their tickets, thanked Jack for the ride, took their bags, and boarded the train. Jim Henry carried some extra clothing, a sharp knife, his Bible, and Julia's picture, along with food prepared and packed by Eunice. Their coach was not full until the train reached Greensboro, where it was attached to a larger train coming up from the south. The next day, after many stops, they arrived at the Pennsylvania Railroad's terminus at Exchange Place in Jersey City, New Jersey. All Manhattan-bound passengers had to get off the train and board a ferry for the last portion of their journey. There was not yet a railroad bridge or tunnel across the Hudson River into New York City.

As the steam ferry crossed the Hudson, Jim Henry and Nate looked in amazement at the river traffic, the many docks and warehouses along the river, and the tall buildings beyond. They noted the locations of ocean-going vessels. Most of them were steamers with side paddle wheels and stubby masts for supplemental sail power. The sailing ships were easy to spot. Their masts stood so tall that some of their tops were lost in the rising patches of morning fog. The ferry Jim Henry and Nate boarded headed for a dock in lower Manhattan near the battery, which consisted of fortified naval gun emplacements. There were many ocean-going vessels docked nearby along the Hudson River.

As they neared the dock, Jim Henry and Nate hurried toward the gangway in order to be among the first ones off. Jim Henry asked a fellow passenger standing next to him if he knew where they could find a cheap hotel. The passenger said, "The Bowery has cheap hotels, but the area is pretty rough. It is down to the right."

Jim Henry decided to initiate their job search with the ships just north of the ferry landing, with the idea of working their way south toward the Bowery. First, they tried the steamers and found that they were run by large companies that already had crews lined up, and would only offer to place their names on a waiting list for a future interview. Next, they turned to the largest of the sailing ships, tall square-riggers covered with complex masts and ropes. They approached a particularly large one and asked a crewman where it was headed. The crewman responded, "Panama."

"You need some more hands?"

"Come on up. The mate may wish to talk with you."

Jim Henry and Nate climbed aboard and were greeted by a bearded first mate, who spoke with a British accent. "What is your experience?"

"It's been mostly farming and a bit of soldiering," said Jim Henry.

"You sound like a Southerner. You guys can't be all bad. You have any problem with heights?"

"I don't think I have a problem. I've been up many a tree."

"Show me how fast you can get to the top of that mast. It's 155 feet."

Jim Henry looked at the main mast, which seemed to stretch

to the heavens, and realized that there was no ladder. He swung his eyes to the side and saw that the heavy rope shrouds that held the mast vertical had horizontal ropes laced between them so a person could climb up. He went right up until he came to a crow's nest about fifty feet up. To go further, he had to climb up into the crow's nest and then reach out to grab onto a set of smaller lines going up to the cross timber at the top of the sails. Near the top, the lines came together in a space so narrow he could barely wedge his toes into them.

Then he had to reach out and pull himself up on another set of lines leading to the top of the royal yard, to which the top of the uppermost sail would be attached. When there were no ropes going any higher, Jim Henry looked down in triumph. He could see the outline of the entire ship below him. It seemed small in the 155-foot vertical distance. He looked out over the view of New York and saw that he was higher than all the buildings, except for the spire of a nearby church. It was a beautiful stone structure. He was impressed that the tallest building in New York City was a church.

Jim Henry continued to look with amazement on the city with its rivers and buildings stretching as far as he could see. His gaze followed New York Harbor all the way to the ocean.

Just then the first mate shouted, "Why are you stopping? Get on up to the top."

Jim Henry looked above him and there was nothing but a thin bare mast standing eight feet above his head. So he shinnied up, just as though he were shinnying up a tree to shake out a possum, and placed his hand on the very top of the mast.

As he descended, Jim Henry thought the climb was dangerous enough with the ship tied to the dock, but that it would be quite another matter to be sent aloft to furl or unfurl huge sails as they snapped in the wind and as the ship rolled and tossed in high waves. He also thought of Julia and her admonishment for him to "keep safe." In Jim Henry's eyes, it would take a lot of money to justify signing on with this ship.

"We'll take you," the mate said, "but with no sea experience we cannot pay you anything in addition to your bunk, your food, and your transport. You'll pull watch just like everyone else."

Jim Henry and Nate exchanged looks. The terms did not suit either of them.

Jim Henry said, "Thank you for your kind offer. If we are not being paid, we might find a smaller ship more suitable. Sorry to trouble you."

The mate replied, "You might check with some of those schooners over there. I expect you'll find one bound for Panama. Good luck."

———◆———

Jim Henry and Nate headed toward the area where the schooners were docked, and after several inquiries, they found one about to set sail for Panama with a load of calves. It was a topsail schooner named the Dark Star, captained by a distinguished-looking forty-year-old with a weathered face that bespoke much time at sea. In talking with the captain about employment, they found that their farm experience was quite an asset, because none of the crew members thus far hired knew how to handle cattle. Upon learning of their desire for passage to California, the captain said that Jim Henry and Nate could serve as crewmen primarily responsible for the care of 300 calves, not only on the trip to Panama, but also for the train trip across the Isthmus and then on another ship to San Francisco, with that captain's permission. Their pay would be their meals and free passage. Their principal job would be loading and unloading the feeder calves, feeding and watering them, and forking out their waste. They would not be assigned to a watch at sea, but they were expected to respond to "all hands on deck" calls to help man the ship in case of need.

The captain then introduced them to the first mate, who appeared to be in his thirties and exuded competence and confidence, and the second mate, who appeared to be in his twenties and said little and shifted his weight nervously from foot to foot. The captain explained, "This is his first voyage as second mate, but he's a good seaman and will be working under my close supervision."

Jim was surprised at the apparent difference between the experience levels of the first and second mate. He knew which of the two he would stay close to, to learn the skills he'd need as a seaman.

The first mate then took Jim Henry and Nate to the forecastle, pronounced fo'c'sle, where the rest of the crew slept and kept their gear. The wooden structure was about twenty feet square, built on the deck just on the bow side of the fore mast. There was a partition running down the center of it and in each of the two sub-compartments were three double deck bunks.

The mate said, "The port side is for the port watch and starboard for the starboard watch. You two, the cook, and the ship's carpenter will not be assigned to a watch. You can split up however you like, port or starboard."

Jim Henry asked, "Why not just say right and left?"

The mate replied, "Left and right depend on where you are and which way you are looking. Starboard has meant the right side of a vessel ever since the early Norse ships had a steering board that functioned like a rudder on the right-hand side of the aft part of the ship. Starboard meant steering board. With the steering board stuck out on the right side, the ship had to come up against the wharf with its left side toward the port. That's how it got to be called port. Use the right words and let folks know you are a sailor."

"When do we start work?" asked Nate.

"The cook puts out breakfast at six in the morning, and we'll start loading right after that. You can sleep on the ship tonight, but you'll need to find your own supper. There are plenty of places to eat in the Bowery. In the meantime, we will need you to sign the crew agreement. Come with me to the office."

The mate led them down to the wharf and about a block along the adjacent street to the owner-manager's office. There they were shown an agreement and account of crew. In bold print near the top of the agreement was the legend "No spirits and no cursing allowed." Jim Henry wondered at the possibility of enforcing such a rule with sailors, but felt that the rule spoke well for the owners and might be a good influence on the men. The agreement reflected the terms of employment of each crew member, down to the amount of food and water to be furnished to each man each day. Jim Henry's and Nate's responsibilities for tending the cattle remained in effect until the cargo was unloaded in San Francisco, while the other crew members were obligated to remain with the ship until it returned to New York. The owners of the ship had an arrangement with a California-based shipping company for their ships to make their runs to Panama on coordinated schedules so they could pick up each other's cargo and offer continuous cargo service both ways between New York and San Francisco. Jim Henry noticed the part of the crew agreement that said, "Length of voyage not to exceed six months," and inquired, "Why so long a time?"

"The voyage to Panama should take less than a month, the trip across the isthmus less than a day, and the voyage to San Francisco less than a month. You may have to wait a few days to make connections. The owners just cannot afford to have everyone jump ship in case of an unavoidable delay."

The mate's signature was already on the same agreement, and Jim Henry and Nate added theirs.

Jim Henry and Nate decided to use the remaining hours of daylight to look around the city and find a place to eat supper. As they headed toward the Bowery, they came upon the church that Jim Henry had seen from the top of the mast of the square-rigger. It was Trinity Church, located at the corner of Broadway and Wall Street. From the sign in front of the church they learned that George Washington had worshipped in the original church at that site when he was president and the capitol of the United States was New York City. They went inside and learned that the church they stood in was completed in 1846. They also confirmed what Jim Henry already knew, that the 281-foot spire was the tallest structure in New York.

As they entered the Bowery, the run-down state of homes and buildings that had once been elegant showed how far the section had fallen from its glory days.

Jim Henry and Nate picked out a restaurant that looked decent and seemed to be well patronized by sailors. The prices were so high that they decided to split a meal and supplement it later with the food they had left from home. Their waitress had a provocative manner about her as she flaunted her short dress and a low neckline. Toward the end of the meal she asked if they would like to visit with her later on. She had not finished getting the words out of her mouth when Jim Henry said, "No thank you."

As the waitress walked away, Nate, who appreciated the tempting swivel of her ample hips, asked, "How could you dismiss her so quickly?"

"It was easy," Jim Henry said as he pulled the framed daguerreotype of Julia out of his breast pocket. "The only reason I am making this trip is to earn enough money in California for us to get married."

"Well, my situation is different. At least we could have checked out her price," Nate said.

"We'd best be getting back to the ship. Six o'clock is going to come mighty early," Jim Henry said, and they left the restaurant and the Bowery.

Before drifting off to sleep that night, Jim Henry thanked the Lord for their quick success in finding transportation to San Francisco. He prayed that the voyage to Panama would be a good one and that the Lord would bless and keep Julia safe.

16

Voyage to Panama

*A*t breakfast, the captain stood and addressed the crew. "Gentle-men, get accustomed to the company of the men around you. Before long you will be bonded like brothers. You have been chosen for this trip because of the skills you have to offer. Some have different skills than others, and I encourage you to share your skills with your fellow crew members and to be quick to ask about things others can teach you. We must all work together as a team. The owners have charged me with the command of this ship with the request that I act as though the ship were mine and uninsured. I encourage each of you to be similarly mindful of the responsibility we share for the ship, its cargo, and most especially your fellow crewmen. It is now time to choose the watches."

The mate, as leader of the port watch, and the second mate, as leader of the starboard watch, took turns picking the men who would staff their respective watches. The more experienced seamen were chosen first. Soon all the seamen had been chosen, leaving only the cook, the carpenter, Jim Henry, and Nate.

The captain announced, "By tradition the cook is assigned to the port watch, and the carpenter is responsible solely to me, but is on the starboard watch under the first mate when all hands are needed on deck. The same goes for our two cattle handlers. Jim Henry Shore and Nate Poindexter will work with the cattle under my direction, but when all hands are needed, Jim Henry will be on the port watch and Nate will be on the starboard watch."

Jim Henry at first was disappointed he was not placed on the starboard watch, because he liked the first mate who would head it and wanted to be on his team. Then the captain continued, "The starboard watch will be responsible for loading half the feed, straw, and cattle through the forward hatch and the port watch will be responsible for loading the other half of the provisions and animals through the aft hatch."

Jim Henry then recognized that being on the port watch placed him near the poop deck, where he would be in close proximity to both the second mate and the captain. He and Nate both were pleased to be reporting directly to the captain.

The loading process went smoothly. The port was equipped with cranes with power winches and hydraulically controlled booms. The hay, corn, and straw were placed in slings and hoisted onto the ship and lowered through two large hatches to the hold below. The hold of the Dark Star had a second floor built between the bottom and top of the hold to double the area where livestock could be secured in place. Attached to the floor were rows of rings to which the calves would be tethered in order to guard against the possibility of the load shifting during the voyage.

Jim Henry, Nate, and other crew members under the direction of the mate piled the corn and hay into large compartments at the bow and stern end of each floor and spread the bedding straw throughout the remaining space on both levels. Each level of the hold had no more than five feet of headspace, which was enough for calves that had just been weaned, but not enough room for a man to stand erect. The lack of head space and the necessity of working in a hunched over position soon became uncomfortable, and for some it was painful.

It was a dusty job, and some of the men were soon coughing and wheezing, even with wet handkerchiefs stretched across their faces. The men were wet with perspiration and the dust stuck to them. The dust caked their handkerchiefs and got in their eyes.

After two hours of hauling feed and spreading hay, the men's backs were getting sore. Several men said they could stand it no longer and asked for permission to leave the hold, and he heard the mate's reaction: "Get back in there and finish the job, this is the worst part and you are almost done!" By noon, the fodder, corn, and straw were all in place.

As the crew gathered at the galley to pick up their noon meal, the captain directed their attention across the Hudson to a cattle barge and steam tug heading their way from the Jersey City side of the Hudson.

"Gentlemen," he said, "those appear to be our cattle—our payload. Our job this afternoon is to get them safely off the barge and into the hold. Our carpenter set up pulleys and rope above each hatch for lowering these calves to the hold. Make sure each calf is well secured in the sling. Each calf will have a rope around its neck. Once it's in the hold, you lead it forward and secure it to a ring in the floor. Start with the rings farthest from the hatch and work back toward the hatch. If you have trouble with an animal, call for Jim Henry or Nate."

Soon the cattle barge was tied alongside and the barge's crew began to drive the calves up chutes from the barge's deck to the Dark Star's deck. Crew members led the calves to the hatches, fastened slings around them, and lowered each calf into the hold. On each floor below, men led each calf to a ring and tied it with just enough slack to allow it to stand or lie down.

Seeing all these calves tethered to the floor in such close quarters caused Jim Henry to think of slaves being chained down in slave ships. He had heard of the famous case of the Amistad, a schooner whose cargo of slaves took over the ship. He wondered if the Dark Star had ever been a slaver.

"Jim Henry, on deck!" the second mate bellowed. Jim Henry climbed the ladder out of the hold at the aft hatch and found three men holding down a calf thrashing on the deck.

"Get me a bucket of corn," Jim Henry said. He stripped off his shirt and tied it around the calf's head to cover its eyes. He stroked the calf and spoke to it, "Sukkee, sukkee, sukkee." Pretty soon the thrashing stopped, and Jim Henry let it stand and eat corn from the bucket while he slid the sling under its belly. As the calf was being lowered into the hold, Jim Henry went back down the ladder and led the calf to its place and tied it, only to hear more commotion up top.

As he scrambled up the ladder, Jim Henry could tell calves were getting rambunctious at both hatches and several ran free.

"Don't let any more on board until we get them under control," Jim Henry called to the second mate. "Hold out a bucket of corn for the loose ones and while they are eating tether them here on the deck. We'll take them below starting with the most settled ones."

Soon all 300 calves were either tethered below or on deck. Jim Henry advised the captain it would be easier to get the most difficult one below if they waited until after dark. The captain issued that order, then told the crew they had an hour to clean up and eat.

The cook served up pork, bread, and peas for supper. "Enjoy this soft bread while it lasts. Soon we'll be down to the hard tack."

One seaman replied, "Hard tack isn't bad if you knock it against something hard to get the weevils out of it."

Another seaman said, "You don't really have to do that. A bit of extra protein won't hurt you!"

Jim Henry thought about the food provisions in the crew agreement and could not recall that it said anything about hard tack or weevils—it only covered the staples of yams or potatoes, flour or rice, salt meat, peas and water. And he thought about his year in prison and how precious a bit of stale bread was, even with weevils.

As darkness settled over New York Harbor on December 15,

1868, the captain called, "All hands on deck!" Jim Henry took his place with the port crew. There were no lighted lanterns on the deck of the Dark Star and the darkness was almost absolute with no moon and little light from the few city gas lights near the water front. No stars were visible through the smoke of the heating season.

Jim Henry and Nate led the efforts to get the last calves into the holds. When the last ones were tied in place, the captain ordered, "Starboard watch prepare to secure the tow line. Port watch, prepare to cast off."

A side wheeler steam tug was coming along side. In a few minutes, the Dark Star eased out into the Hudson River and New York Harbor. Jim Henry said a prayer of thanks that he'd found his way to California and asked God's continued blessings for himself, his family, and Julia. Then he gave way to his excitement. His future, like the schooner, was finally underway.

He stayed on deck for the next two hours, even though he had no work to do. He wanted to see everything that happened. They were under tow through the harbor and out through the Narrows to the ocean. Although the tug was responsible for navigation, the Dark Star's captain stayed on the poop deck the whole way and called for a double lookout because of the traffic in and around the shipping channel. There were red lights, green lights, and white lights moving across the water in almost every direction. As the ship passed though the Narrows, no more than two miles wide, shore lights were clearly visible on both sides.

As they cleared the Narrows, the captain called, "All hands on deck to set sail." The starboard watch gathered at the fo'c'sle and the port watch just in front of the poop deck.

Now Jim Henry had a job to do, and that was to manage the cattle on board the ship. When it came to sailing the vessel, Jim Henry did his best to help the rest of the crew and to stay out of the way when the sailing chores exceeded his expertise. He followed his fellow seaman. It was obvious that everyone knew exactly where to be and what to do. If there was any doubt, the second mate relayed orders from the captain. Jim Henry did his best to keep up, to stay out of the way, and to not be a hindrance.

As the Dark Star's crew pulled on the halyards to raise the sails, the tug captain slowed down and signaled for the hawser to be released. Then he turned about and gave a couple of friendly toots from his whistle as he passed by on his way back to New York.

The helmsman rang eight bells to mark the change of a watch. As the vibrations following the last ring died away, Jim Henry thought how the bell gave a sense of time and place to those on the vessel. The number of rings told them the time and the fact that there was no echo answering back told him that they were now in their own world with nothing around them to reflect the sound. The motion of the ship was unfamiliar to him. The sounds around him were unfamiliar. The men called back and forth in the language of their world, one he was only beginning to understand.

Jim Henry and Nate turned in early that night. Their job was to work all day, feeding and watering 300 calves and forking out their manure. The calves would be hungry, thirsty, and restless. They had to be ready to work at first light.

Right after breakfast, Jim Henry and Nate climbed down into the hold as morning was beginning to break. The calves were indeed restless. The men worked from each end of the lower floor and then the upper floor. They dragged hay bundled in canvas along the passageway and used pitch forks to put a small pile of hay in front of each calf. Then they drew water from large casks and carried it bucket by bucket to the calves. As they waited for the calves to drink, they used their pitch forks to fork manure out of the straw to be thrown overboard. The work taxed their backs, as they could not stand up straight.

Daylight did not penetrate the hold, so when Jim Henry and

Nate climbed up to the deck just before noon, they were startled by the bright sunlight. The square topsail had been set and the captain and second mate were on the poop deck shooting the sun with the sextant. The captain would call out the degrees, minutes, and seconds separating the sun from the horizon, and the mate would write down each reading and the chronometer time of each mark, down to the second.

Jim Henry watched as they looked at the data and interpolated to determine the exact time of the sun's zenith and the angle of the sun from the horizon at that time, from which they determined the Dark Star's latitude and longitude. He wanted to ask for explanations but knew his superiors wouldn't welcome the interruption. He had to learn by listening and piecing information together for himself.

The captain studied the chart for a moment. "We should pass Cape May by dark." He turned to the helmsman and told him to hold a course south by southwest. Then he saw Jim Henry and seemed to read the questions in his mind. "We give up a couple of knots of speed heading slightly into the wind, but we can more than make up for it by riding a southerly current instead of fighting a northerly one."

That afternoon, Jim Henry and Nate went back into the hold, and for the next several hours busied themselves with forking up manure so the calves would not be sleeping in their own excrement.

As Jim Henry worked, he thought of the contrast between the care and attention given to the calves and stories he had heard from Reverend Bond and other Quakers of the treatment of human beings chained naked in the holds of slave ships with insufficient food and water and no waste removal.

Jim Henry and Nate were uncomfortable as they worked in the low cramped quarters, and they learned to do their work faster and more efficiently in order to get out of the hold sooner. They finished their work well in advance of the evening meal and had an opportunity to visit with other crewmen who were beginning to gather at the galley. Most of them were between twenty and thirty years old, and a few, like Jim Henry and Nate, were in their early twenties and even fewer were older than thirty. They came from various backgrounds and most had been to grade school. Most all of them had been to sea and some were veterans of many voyages. Several, in addition to Jim Henry and Nate had grown up on farms. All of them but Jim Henry and Nate were from the Northeast.

Jim Henry observed to no one in particular, "I wonder if this ship used to carry slaves."

"Could be," remarked one of the older seamen, "but if so, it was a long time ago."

"As I recall, the Amistad was a topsail schooner just like this one," an older seaman said. "I heard it was sold. It could still be in use under a different name."

"Such as the Dark Star?" said Jim Henry. "There are a lot of tie-down rings below."

"There are so many thousands of schooners in this part of the world that there's a mighty small chance that this schooner was ever the Amistad."

After supper, men began looking to starboard for the Cape May lighthouse. At first, the last glimmers of sunset in the west interfered with their efforts, but as total darkness fell, Jim Henry saw a pinpoint of light flashing every fifteen seconds on the distant horizon. As it receded out of sight, Jim Henry felt a detachment from the world he had known. He instinctively reached for Julia's daguerreotype. Although he could not see it in the dark, he held it close to his heart and thought of her and how much he was already missing her.

Two days later, on December 18, 1868, Jim Henry was able to see yet another lighthouse along the coast. It was daytime and from several miles out, he could see the candy stripe pattern of black and white markings that denoted North Carolina's Cape Hatteras lighthouse.

At this point the captain ordered the helmsman to swing the Dark Star from a southerly course to a course of south by southeast, which would take it across the Gulf Stream and to the Windward Passage between Cuba and Haiti.

This change in direction aligned the Dark Star more closely with the prevailing westerly wind, and the captain called, "All hands on deck to set the topsail." The schooner was soon under full sail and gently rolled with the swells as it cut through the water.

Jim Henry turned his attention back to the Cape Hatteras lighthouse. It was now directly astern and so far away he could barely see it. He watched it until it disappeared in the distant haze. Again, his thoughts were drawn back to home and to Julia. Soon they would be farther away from each other than they had ever been. Jim Henry mused to himself that the previous lengthy periods of separation from Julia he'd already endured were good preparation for this one. He had no doubt that their love would stand the test. Jim Henry paused to pray for Julia and their relationship during this farthest separation they had experienced.

Jim Henry was snapped out of his reverie by the lookout's shout, "Gulf Stream ahead!" Jim Henry looked ahead and could see a distinct line where the ocean changed from gray-blue to a lighter greenish-blue. Just as Jim Henry was thinking how nice it was to be topside and able to see the Dark Star's progress through the ocean, Nate Poindexter nudged him and said, "We'd best get on down below so we can finish by supper."

Jim Henry did not like having to work below deck during the daylight hours, not only because he would miss some sights up top, but also because he missed the camaraderie of the larger group of crewmen working topside. A deal is a deal, he thought, and he would not be heard to complain.

After the first few days at sea, the crew of the Dark Star had begun to settle into a routine. Jim Henry saw that the seamen had a lot of variety in their work, going from one talk to another, no two watches exactly the same. It was not the same for himself and Nate, but the more he thought about it, they also went from job to job—feeding, watering, and cleaning up manure. He decided it was not the work that was the problem; the problem was not having the opportunity to work with the crew as a whole and enjoy their companionship while on duty.

Jim Henry would from time-to-time volunteer to help the watch on duty after supper and before retiring for the evening. His favorite job was that of helmsman. The compass, encased in a lighted binnacle, would swing back and forth as the ship rolled with the waves and swells, while a star served as a steady reference point. The action of the sails provided another reference point for the helmsman. There needed to be a smooth airflow across the sails. If any of them failed to pull smoothly, either the vessel was off course or the wind had changed. Either condition called for corrective action.

Jim Henry thought of the difficulty of the captain's job of being responsible for the ship and crew twenty-four hours a day. During daylight hours, the captain could usually be found on the poop deck, checking the sails, watching for signs of a weather change, taking sextant readings at noon each day and simply observing the crew members on duty. He was accessible to crewmen, and Jim Henry enjoyed visiting with him and learning more about handling a sailing vessel at sea.

—◆—

After two good days of sailing, the westerly wind gradually died down until the Dark Star was just ghosting along on a calm sea. The mate told Jim Henry and Nate that they were now in the horse latitudes, where winds are very light and variable in direction.

Jim Henry asked the mate, "How long is this situation likely to last?"

"Nobody knows, the wind could pick up tomorrow or we could stay becalmed for days."

Jim Henry asked, "What does 'horse latitude' mean?"

"It is a band of latitude that lies between the prevailing wester-lies on the north and the trade winds to the south. There are horse latitudes in the southern hemisphere, too, between the trades and the westerlies."

"But why are they called horse latitudes?"

"The horse latitudes do not have much rain. The Spanish in olden times would bring horses to the New World. It is said that they were once becalmed in these latitudes and were running out of water. In order to save water for themselves, they threw the horses overboard."

For the next two days, the Dark Star barely made enough speed to steer. Most of the steering had to be accomplished by constant-ly adjusting the sails, as there was not enough water speed for the rudder to have much effect. Jim Henry remembered a poem he had read in school, The Rime of the Ancient Mariner, "Water, wa-ter everywhere, nor any a drop to drink." He wondered if anyone had actually thrown horses overboard to save water.

On the third day, the men could see high clouds coming from the east, and an easterly breeze began to blow. It wasn't much at first, but it rose to ten knots and lifted everyone's spirits as the Dark Star resumed her course to the south.

The following day was Christmas Eve, and as the crew was fin-ishing the evening meal, Jim Henry said to them, "Since tomor-row is Christmas would you like for me to read the Christmas story from Luke 2?"

"Read it!" several men answered.

Jim Henry read the first twenty verses. As he finished, a seaman stood and began to sing carols. The crew joined in and Jim Henry thought he'd never had such a fine Christmas.

The next afternoon, December 25, 1868, the lookout called, "Land ho! Merry Christmas everybody!"

Jim Henry and Nate hurried to finish their afternoon's work with the calves, and when they finally arrived on deck, they saw crew members on deck straining to see what the lookout had seen from aloft. An island was just then becoming visible at deck level.

"Gentlemen," the captain said, "you are looking at the first land that Christopher Columbus saw in 1492 on his first trip to the New World. That island is San Salvador, where he landed." The captain showed Jim Henry his chart, which showed San Salvador exactly on the course from Cape Hatteras to the Windward Passage.

Jim Henry was impressed that the captain could navigate accurately enough to hit this tiny speck of land, after sailing seven days and some eight hundred miles from the previous landfall of Cape Hatteras.

Within two hours the Dark Star passed by the eastern side of San Salvador, one of the Bahamas archipelago of several thousand islands and cays, a cay being a small low-level sandy island formed on a base of coral reef.

By the time San Salvador disappeared astern, the sun was low in the western sky. The captain called for all hands on deck. "Gentlemen," he said, "tonight we plan to pass between Crooked Island and Long Cay seventy miles to the south and about twenty miles apart. We have a full moon to help us. To make sure we hit the passage between the islands, we will have a double lookout and two men on the helm at all times to maintain a course of exactly due south. The wind drift to the west should put us directly between the islands. Finally, before it gets dark, we need to take down the topsail in order to be in position to do some quick ma-neuvering during the night."

As the seamen were taking down and furling the topsail, Jim Henry and Nate remained on the poop deck with the captain, who explained, "Long Cay, which was once known as Fortune Is-land, is another place where Columbus stopped. It was home to some forty cotton plantations and 1,200 slaves until 1836, when slavery was abolished. It will be to starboard and Crooked Island to port. Then in another fifty miles we will come to Acklin Island, which has a lighthouse first put into service this year. Without it, I would hesitate to approach these islands at night, but with the full moon, the lighthouse, and care in holding our heading, we'll be all right."

That night, as Jim Henry went to the fo'c'sle to get some sleep, he heard one of the seamen grumbling that the Dark Star had no business sailing in Bahaman waters at night.

"There's too much shallow water and too many coral reefs," the man said. "The captain is pushing too hard. He must be try-ing to make up for some of those three days we lost in the horse latitudes, so we don't have to put into one of these islands to take on more water."

Jim Henry had enough confidence in the captain to go to sleep without worry.

At dawn the next morning, Jim Henry found his confidence to be justified, as he watched the Dark Star pass by the east side of Acklin Island and its new lighthouse, which, as expected, was sending out two white flashes every twenty seconds. The next landfall would be Great Inagua, the third largest island of the Ba-hamas, almost a hundred miles to the southeast.

Late that afternoon as Jim Henry and Nate were climbing up from their work in the hold, they heard the lookout calling, "Land ho!"

They watched as the island came into view, and they passed by its western side shortly before sundown. The captain was pleased to have passed by in daylight, as Great Inagua Island did not yet have a lighthouse. He was also pleased to be able to swing from a south-by-southeasterly to a south-by-southwesterly course, which would enable them to take better advantage of the easterly trade winds. Just before dark he ordered the topsail to be set.

The Dark Star was now in the Windward Passage, a stretch of deep water in the triangle formed by Great Inagua Island, the eastern tip of Cuba, and the northwestern tip of Haiti on the island of Hispaniola. The passage between Cuba and Haiti was fifty miles wide and posed no night navigation problem. The next morning Jim Henry could see the mountains of Haiti and Cuba on the horizon as the Dark Star made its way south toward the wide passage between the eastern end of Jamaica and the southwestern peninsula of Haiti.

For the next four days, the Dark Star continued its south-by-southwesterly course across an 800-mile stretch of the Caribbean Sea to the Republic of Panama. Two rain squalls broke the normal shipboard routine. Out of an abundance of caution the captain ordered the topsail furled.

The rain required the temporary closing of the hatches to the hold so that Jim Henry and Nate had to work in the dark. By this time, a few of the calves were beginning to look weak and sickly. Jim Henry and Nate fed those calves a diet of corn, which seemed to strengthen them. Then they gave extra feed to all the calves in preparation for landing and the possibility of missing the regular feeding time.

17
Panama

On January 3, 1869, the lookout called, "Land ho!" The Dark Star was approaching its destination of Aspinwall, the Atlantic terminus of the railroad across the isthmus of Panama. North Americans who founded the town in 1850 named it in honor of William Henry Aspinwall, a founder and promoter of the Panama Railroad Company.

The crew helped Jim Henry and Nate hoist the calves out of the hold. A shipper representative from the owner-agent's office in Panama appeared and arranged for the calves to be loaded onto cattle cars along with the remainder of their feed. Jim Henry asked the agent how long the train trip would take.

"Two or three hours," the man said. "By the way, you two ride with the calves."

Jim Henry and Nate looked at each other and laughed. "I guess we must smell enough like them, nobody wants us in a passenger car," Jim Henry said.

As the train rolled along, Jim Henry saw dense jungles, impenetrable forests, a mountain range, a roaring river, and smaller streams with heavy foliage overhanging them. Never had he seen such an array of brightly colored birds, some of them quite large, nor had he seen so many orchids and other beautiful flowers growing in the wild. When he got off the boat, he saw the native people looking poor and tired; he was intrigued with the contrast between pitiful circumstances of the native population, which seemed desperately poor, ill clad, and living in primitive hovels, and the magnificent and verdant landscape all along the rail line.

Within three hours, they crossed the isthmus and arrived in Panama City. The cattle cars were detached from the train and parked on a siding. Jim Henry and Nate spent the rest of the afternoon feeding and watering the animals in a stockyard. They were glad to find a bunk house for themselves.

That night, they went to a small local restaurant and enjoyed fresh seafood. The next morning, they learned that the ship was still not in, so they fed and watered the calves and went to the marketplace to get some food. They were beset on every side with tradespeople calling loudly in Spanish and occasionally in English, touting all kinds of merchandise, including tropical fruit, birds, monkeys, wood carvings, and beautiful seashells.

One young merchant showed Jim Henry a particularly large, heavy conch shell with a smooth, round hole cut in the center of its face to allow the shell to serve as a trumpet. It was gracefully formed with a cream-colored exterior and pink interior. The young man raised the shell to his lips and blew it with a reverberating roar. Jim Henry tried it until he could do the same thing.

When the young man said, "Only four dollars." Jim Henry laughed and said, "One dollar!" The young man handed Jim Henry the shell and said, "Two dollars."

Jim Henry gave it back and began to walk away.

The young man shouted, "Amigo." Jim Henry turned back to see the young man smiling, holding out the shell and saying, "For you, one dollar." Jim Henry knew he was down to his last few dollars, but he also knew Panama was the farthest from home he was likely ever to travel and he wanted a souvenir to show he had been there. Jim Henry parted with a dollar and tucked the shell under his arm, thinking how Julia would marvel at it.

During the next two days Jim Henry and Nate worked with the calves. The owner-agent had provided new feed and the calves didn't like it. A few refused to eat it at all and were rapidly losing weight. Jim Henry and Nate identified those animals and fed them a mixture of the old hay and grain. By their estimate, there was enough old hay left from the original load of feed to sustain those who refused the new hay.

On the third day in Panama City, their ship came in. It was larger than the Dark Star and had enough headroom room for a person to stand on each of the two floors of the hold. Jim Henry and Nate were thrilled they would not have to work stooped over all the time. They were further pleased at the ease with which they and the ship's crew were able load the calves. No doubt it helped that the calves had become more accustomed to being lifted with a sling, but the main difference was that they had become used to Jim Henry and Nate, who had been feeding them for more than three weeks.

18
The Pacific

The cattle ship departed Panama City on a favorable easterly breeze. The ship stayed closer to the shore and Jim Henry watched the coastlines of Costa Rica, Nicaragua, Honduras, Guatemala, and Mexico flow by. Then they tacked northwestward, out of sight of land until they reached California.

—◆—

One afternoon, Jim Henry heard the lookout call, "Thar she blows!" Jim Henry ran forward, climbed on top of the forecastle, and saw a pod of whales in the distance. At first, he could see only spouts of water vapor and the flicks of huge tails as the animals dove. As the ship drew closer, he could see the vast length of their bodies. The captain changed course to bring the ship very close to the whales, and Jim Henry was able to pick out a mother and calf swimming and diving together. They would dive together, and after a short interval, the calf would come back to the surface. After what seemed like an eternity, the mother would pop back up right next to the calf. She must have had her eye on the calf the whole time she was away. Instinctively, Jim Henry opened Julia's locket as if to share the experience with her. How he wished she were here with him. How he wished he could, like the mother whale, keep his beloved in sight the whole time he was away. As the whales passed astern and the ship continued seaward, Jim Henry went back to work. His exhilaration lasted a long time, and the prospect of sharing it with Julia was an escape from the confines of the hold.

The next day as he worked in the hold, he heard and felt another change in the rhythm of the ship that showed it was encountering large swells. Soon came the call, "All hands on deck." On the captain's orders, the crew struck all sails except for two jibs and the spanker. For the next two days, the ship fought gale winds and heavy seas. The constant motion kept many of the calves from eating hay. Jim Henry and Nate checked each calf and offered rations of grain to the weakest ones, but some refused to eat even grain.

The heavy winds and seas finally subsided, but several calves were unable to stand. Hardly had calm seas returned when rain started again and another gale ensued. What had been full-time work in feeding, watering, and clearing out manure had become more than full time, because of the care required to save the distressed calves.

By the time the second gale subsided, Jim Henry and Nate were totally exhausted from heavy work and little sleep. They considered themselves fortunate for losing only a few calves, which they sent to the galley for the cook to butcher and serve.

After three weeks at sea, the headlands around San Francisco loomed in the distance. By late afternoon they had drawn close enough to see that much of the shoreline and the entire entrance to San Francisco Bay was enshrouded by fog. Accordingly, the captain decided to heave to for the night and ordered all sails but a jib on the foremast and the spanker on the mizzen mast to be taken down.

At dinner that night, crew members talked about how they could not wait to get to the Barbary Coast, which seemed to have plenty of bars, flop houses, and cheap eateries for visiting sailors, and was rife with prostitution and gambling. Jim Henry learned that it even had opium dens, run by residents of nearby

Chinatown, the largest population of Chinese outside China. With the name from the North African Coast and the aura of a Muslim paradise, the Barbary Coast consisted of a nine-block area extending from the center of San Francisco toward the bay. Since San Francisco was a favorite place for sailors to jump ship, there was a perpetual need for seamen, and sailors who got drunk or put themselves in a position to be overpowered were susceptible to being shanghaied. The place reminded Jim Henry of the Bowery he had seen at the foot of Manhattan Island.

Nate asked Jim Henry, "How about our visiting the Barbary Coast before heading for San Jose?"

"No way Nate, I'm down to my last dollar and fifty cents, and I don't aim to spend it at the Barbary Coast. As soon as I hit land, I'm going to be looking for work. When I am able, I will go on to San Jose."

The two decided to part company as they left the ship, and to contact each other later in San Jose through John Henry Hauser, their mutual friend from Yadkin County. Hauser was Jim Henry's age and had volunteered for Confederate Army service at the outset of the war when he was only thirteen years old. In 1867, he had traveled to California by sailing around Cape Horn. Nate and Jim Henry had Hauser's address and planned to look to him for help in finding work in San Jose.

The next morning the fog cleared, and the ship sailed into San Francisco on a westerly wind. The ship turned towards the south to follow the contour of the San Francisco peninsula, passing between the town and Alcatraz Island and turning westward toward the wharves as it passed Yerba Buena Island. It was difficult tacking through heavy boat traffic and soon a steam tug took them in tow toward the wharves. By mid-morning, the ship was docked.

The crew fell to furling sails, swabbing decks, making sure all lines were properly secured, inspecting to see that all belaying pins were in their proper places and generally performing those tasks necessary to leave the ship in shape for its next voyage.

Jim Henry and Nate were not involved in this work. As usual, they spent almost the entire day below deck, where they fed and watered the calves and mucked out waste for what they prayed would be the last time. They went topside to see the Golden Gate entrance to San Francisco Bay, but duties kept them from following the ship's progress as it worked its way through crowded water traffic to its anchorage. They finished their work in the late afternoon and were happy to see a barge with a raised cattle chute tying up alongside the ship. The entire crew pitched in to help them manage the lifting of calves out of the hold and leading them down the cattle chute onto the barge. The calves seemed eager to get off the ship and the transfer of the cattle to the barge went smoothly. Jim Henry was eager to leave, too.

—◆—

Jim Henry did not want to go ashore with the other men or even Nate because most were headed for the Barbary Coast. As a first move, he asked the man in charge of the barge whether he could use an extra hand with the cattle for a day or two. The man knew Jim Henry would be an asset in handling the cattle and said, "Get on the barge!"

Jim Henry asked the captain to release him to accept immediate employment. The captain thanked him for his good work and said that would be fine. Jim Henry thanked the captain for his passage from Panama, and yelled to Nate, "See you in San Jose!"

19

San Jose

The steam tug pushed the barge toward a dock in the southern outskirts of San Francisco. Aboard the barge, Jim Henry met the foreman of a nearby ranch, where the calves' long journey would end. He told the foreman he had been working with the cattle all the way from New York and asked if he could be of useful service in helping to unload and move the cattle to the ranch. He told the foreman he would need a place to stay for a day or two while he looked for a longer-term job. The foreman told him he could live a day or two in the bunk house and eat with the ranch hands while he looked for work.

"What kind of work might there be?" asked Jim Henry. "I'd like to be in San Jose in time for spring planting, but I could work here for a month or so."

"There is a Scotsman nearby who has a good business cutting, splitting, and delivering firewood in San Francisco. He hires extra help during the cold months when people need wood to stay warm. We can put you in touch with him."

As soon as they reached the dock, several men on horseback began to drive the calves toward the ranch. The foreman had one of them get Jim Henry a horse and accompanied him to the home of the Scotsman. After a brief conversation, Mr. McIlroy agreed to hire Jim Henry at a wage of $30 per month and $45 during harvest.

Jim Henry spent February and March splitting and delivering

firewood to McIlroy's customers in San Francisco. By late March, he had enough money for a train ride to San Jose with enough left over for a night in a hotel while he looked for work. As he prepared to leave San Francisco he thanked the Lord for his early success in finding work and prayed for similar success in San Jose.

The ride to San Jose on the Western Pacific Railroad was a pleasant adventure. The rainy season was just ending and it was a beautiful day. As the coach headed south, he could see the high hills of the San Francisco peninsula on the right and the gentle slope down to San Francisco Bay on the left. As the train continued south, the bay gave way to a flat green valley. To Jim Henry, it looked like a huge expanse of river bottomland, miles across and extending out of sight to the south. It was lush with green vegetation, mostly crops, and seemed to be a real paradise for farmers—especially as compared with the uneven and often parched farmland of Yadkin County.

As soon as the train came to a stop at the San Jose station, Jim Henry slung his travel bag over his shoulder and looked for an affordable hotel where he could leave his bag. He did not want to arrive at John Hauser's doorstep with his baggage as though he were expecting to be invited to stay for the night. Once he found a suitable hotel, he asked the clerk for directions and set out on foot toward Hauser's address outside of town. He left the business district, and the residential area through which he was passing gave way to farmland. Soon he made his way to the small farm that Hauser had rented when he came to the area in 1867.

Hauser greeted him warmly. "Welcome to San Jose. I've been looking for you ever since Nate Poindexter came to see me a couple of months ago. I helped him get set up, and hope I can do the same for you."

Jim Henry, who had not seen John for well over a year, was overjoyed. "That would be great! Do you have any leads?"

"You need to go see Jesse Hobson. He and his wife, Sarah, came from North Carolina. They've done very well out here."

"Sounds like a Yadkin County name."

"It is, but I expect they left there before you were born. They got married in Missouri in 1847 and came out here by wagon train. It was the year after the United States acquired California at the end of the Mexican War. He spent two years in the gold mines, where he was very successful. Once, he and his companions were said to have washed out a thousand dollars worth of gold from a single pocket over a period of three days."

"Does he still do any gold mining?"

"No," John said. "He settled in San Jose in 1849 and invested his gold profits in land and farming operations. Back then San Jose was just a little village occupied primarily by Spaniards and Indians living in adobe huts. Land was cheap, and he bought a good bit of it, a large wheat farm and then a nice orchard. His timing was good, because the big gold discovery at Sutter's Mill brought on the gold rush. Over the next few years, hundreds of thousands of people flocked to California and ran up the land prices. Few of them did as well in gold or farming as Jesse Hobson."

"What made farming so profitable?" Jim Henry asked.

"Market conditions out here have been unbelievably favorable. Those '49ers would pay a dollar for a hen egg, and market prices for all kinds of farm products went sky high. This area has good rail and water transport to the markets, good land, and good weather. It is warm enough to get two wheat crops a year."

"How did he know to come out here? Where did he get his information?"

"I guess he was just smart. He was smarter than we were in that he got married and brought his wife out here with him. Women are mighty scarce out here. I plan to go back to North Carolina and marry a good woman. You may need to do the same."

"I've already found a good woman, and I can't wait to go back and marry her. I wish she were already here," Jim Henry said.

"If she's a good woman and you love her, by all means go back, marry her, and bring her back out here. Jesse's wife, Sarah, is a mighty good woman and she loves living here. She was a Spainhour, and her ancestors came from the same part of Switzerland as the Shore family. It seems most people in Yadkin County are kin to each other. I expect her family is related to yours. The subject of family connections reminds me that about ten years ago Jesse helped a William Shore from Yadkin County get started out here. They lived on and ran a farm adjacent to the Hobson farm. William Shore has to be one of your relatives."

"I have an Uncle Bill. He never came out here, but I am sure there are other William Shores in our family."

"In any event, Jesse Hobson is the man to help you. He may even be able to help you set up your own operation. Why don't you spend the night here and we'll take a ride out there tomorrow? I need to go out that way to check on Nate."

"Thanks for your offer, but I have already checked in at a hotel and left my bag there."

"Well, let's go cancel your room and pick up your bag. It's not too late for them to sell the room to someone else."

John hitched up his horse and buggy, and they went to the hotel. The manager agreed to the cancellation, and Jim Henry and John had a leisurely supper in the dining room, Jim Henry's treat. John asked Jim Henry if he would mind telling about his war experiences.

"I don't mind letting people know I enlisted in June 1864 at the age of 17, was captured a week later, and got to spend the last year of the war in a Yankee prisoner of war camp. I saw too much suffering and too many deaths. The worst scenes still come back to me occasionally in my dreams. I try to clear them out of my mind by not thinking or talking about it."

"I am the same way," John said. "I served until the war was over and had just as soon not talk about it. Things stayed so bad after the war that I came out here last year. Are things getting any better back home?"

"Farming is still awful. The military government ended a few months ago, but nobody has any money, and if they raise property taxes to pay for government, there will be even more tax foreclosure sales than we now have. Foreclosure sales are a joke because few have the money to bid. There is not much labor to be had except for family members. The loss of livestock during the war has been compounded by hog cholera. We had three drought seasons in a row, so crops were poor. Hundreds of families haven't had enough grain to make bread, and many haven't had enough even for seed."

"It is a shame so little has changed since I left in 1867. I wanted to go back home this year. The Transcontinental Railroad should be completed this spring and that would make it easy. In fact, people are already riding on the western and eastern portions of it, and Wells Fargo is providing stagecoach service across the gap in Utah where the railroad is incomplete. The only trouble is that it doesn't look like the time is right to be in Yadkin County."

"If Nate and I thought the time was right, we would not be here."

They finished their meal, and the waiter brought the check. After paying the bill, Jim Henry had $2.50 left in his pocket.

That night he thanked the Lord for getting him together with John Hauser and prayed for an equally good meeting with Jesse Hobson.

20

Farming in California

The next day John gave Jim Henry a buggy ride to the Hobson home. Sarah Spainhour Hobson greeted them. She told Jim Henry that, like his Shore ancestors, her Spainhour ancestors had come from the ancient village of Muttenz, Switzerland.

"Maybe we are related," she said. "I'll take you as my long-lost cousin."

He thought, if Sarah could make a home in California, maybe Julia could. And with the Hobsons and John and Nate nearby, he and she could make it feel like Yadkin County.

Sarah pointed them toward the orchard where they might find Jesse. Jim Henry and John found him working in his orchard with two young men, one of whom was his nineteen-year-old son, Thad. The other was a field hand, Virgin Germaine, also nineteen years old.

John Hauser handled the introductions. "Mr. Hobson, meet Jim Henry Shore. He is the friend who traveled from North Carolina with Nate Poindexter."

"Glad you are here," Jesse said. "Are you ready to go to work?"

"Yes sir."

"Right now, we are clearing the weeds and brush out from under these fruit trees. We hope to finish by dinner time. With your help it will be easy. You have work clothes with you?"

"Yes sir."

"Put them on and throw your bags into my wagon."

John Hauser said, "I am going to leave you gentlemen before you put me to work. Jim Henry, if you need anything, you know where to find me."

"John, I appreciate what you have done for me more than I can say."

Jim Henry pitched right in with Jesse, Thaddeus, and Virgin. With Jim Henry's strong help, they finished well before the noon hour and went to the house for dinner.

Jesse told Sarah how he would like to take on Jim Henry as an additional hand. Sarah welcomed Jim Henry aboard, showed him the room he would share with Virgin, and introduced him to their five younger children—William, age eleven, Meary, age ten, Anna, age eight, Martha, age five, and an infant, Sarah.

Jim Henry was struck by the similarity of the Hobson family to his own in the ages and number of children. Just as Jim Henry was two years older than his next oldest brother Aquilla, he was about two years older than the oldest Hobson son, Thad. Jim Henry liked Thad from the outset, perhaps in part because Thad was overjoyed at Jim Henry's arrival. Jim Henry wondered at first whether it was because of his own personal qualities or whether Thad just needed another body to help carry on his father's work.

They sat together at the table, and by the time the meal was over they were well on their way to becoming fast friends. Jim Henry began to feel comfortable in his place with the Hobson family, which already treated him as a member.

After dinner, the men headed out for the afternoon's work. Jim Henry, Jesse, Thad, and Virgin hitched one team of horses to a wagon and another team of horses to a reaping machine. Jim Henry had heard about mechanical reapers but had never seen one in operation. Back home he used a large scythe to cut wheat. It was hard work and he was all for anything that lessened the labor.

Jesse drove the reaper while Jim Henry, Thad, and Virgin alternated between driving the wagon and forking up the wheat, which had been cut on a previous day and left to dry in the field. In a few hours, they loaded beyond the top of the sides. Jesse turned his team away from reaping and back toward the barn.

He let the horses take them back at a slow walk in order not to upset the wagon and its tall load of wheat. They stopped next to a steam-driven threshing machine. Jesse stoked the boiler with firewood and lighted it. While the water in the boiler heated up, the men put the reaper away and released the horses to graze.

Jim Henry was amazed at how fast the threshing machine could separate grain from the straw. Then it dawned on him how much profit could be made by relatively few men working with reaping and threshing machinery to harvest huge acreages of wheat. He also knew that except for a few river bottomlands, the typography of Yadkin County did not lend itself to such large-scale farming. More and more, he saw the opportunities that California offered.

That night he poured out to the Lord his gratitude for bringing him to this place and to this family. Although no specifics had been worked out about economic arrangements, he was confident he would be treated fairly and would have a chance to succeed.

After a week of hard labor with Jesse and Thad, Jim Henry had demonstrated his farming ability and work ethic to the point that Jesse said to him, "You are worth a lot more than the prevailing cash wage rate for farm labor. What about share cropping on a hundred acres of my land? I'll furnish the land, seed, teams, and equipment, and you furnish the labor. At harvest time, we'll split the proceeds of the harvest one third for you and two thirds for me, considering I am taking care of all expenses."

Jim Henry said, "That sounds mighty good to me, but I will miss working along with you and Thad."

"Don't worry one minute about that. Thad and I will want you to continue to help us with our work, and we'll give an equal number of man hours to your work. You may get tired of us, but you are not going to miss us!"

Jim Henry extended his hand and said, "Thank you, sir. I accept with pleasure."

By the end of 1869, Jim Henry earned $1,000. He could see it would take him five years to earn the $5,000 he wanted to accumulate before heading back to Yadkin County. He desperately wanted to cut the time to three years.

In order to get back to Julia as soon as possible, he decided to leverage his work by becoming a cash renter of the land, buying his own animals, equipment, and seed, and paying cash rent for the 150 acres that had been allocated to him. He used 125 acres to grow wheat and the remaining twenty-five acres to grow hay for his horses. As a cash renter, he would be entitled to the entire crop raised on the land.

He knew there was risk. In the event of a poor crop, he would earn less than before and could even lose money because the rent was payable even in the event of total crop failure. However, Jim Henry would not have to share the crop and any profits from the sale of crops would be his. Jesse would receive a smaller fixed return on a smaller capital investment in the operations on the land Jim Henry rented, while Jim Henry would be investing capital and stood to make a larger variable return. Because Jim Henry, Jesse, and Thad worked most of the time as a team, they would work on Jesse's property two days for every day they would work on Jim Henry's 150 acres in order to balance out the man-hours given and received.

As his first capital investment, Jim Henry bought two young horses and a wagon and trained them to pull it. Seeing how adept he was at training horses, Jesse bought two more young horses, which Jim Henry also trained. The next year, Jim Henry bought two more horses, which he used not only on the farm, but also in delivering firewood with Thad's help during the winter. Jim Henry's occupation was documented by the federal census taker in 1870 as "teaming," which signified that handling teams of horses was an important part of Jim Henry's work.

Both Jim Henry and Thad were interested in owning and operating their own farms, and both were working hard to achieve that end. They worked well together and made a good team, although it sometimes seemed they were trying to outdo each other. One day Jesse exclaimed, "I used to have to wake people up around here, and now you two beat me out of bed and are heading for the barn before I can get my work clothes on!"

Jim Henry was usually awake well before the five dongs from the mantlepiece clock signified it was the waking hour. The clock stood two-and-a-half feet tall and was powered by two heavy weights, one for the clock and one for the chimes. Jesse wound the weights up from near the bottom to the top of their line of travel every Sunday. Jim Henry was fascinated by the clock. One day he opened the clock's door, read the operating instructions printed inside and made note of the fact that the instrument was manufactured by the Ansonia Brass and Copper Company of Ansonia, Connecticut. He resolved to purchase one like it one day when he and Julia were settled on their own farm.

It was not just the clock that helped Jim Henry get his day off to an early start. The California climate was so much warmer than North Carolina's in the winter months that he had no need to stay warm in bed until the last possible moment.

But what really propelled him out of the bed was the thought of Julia and the need to earn as much money as he could as soon as he could. By the time the other men were up, Jim Henry would already have a fire going in the wood stove.

After feeding animals and milking cows, the men would return to the house for Sarah's usual big breakfast before heading out at first light with their horses and implements for the morning's work. At noon, they would return to the house for another good meal and then work on the farm until dark. The work schedule was demanding, but no more so than what he had become accustomed to on the farm at home.

The weekly work cycle was broken only by the Sabbath. On Saturday night, everyone would wash up, either in the family wash tub or with a wash pot and wash rag. Jim Henry supplemented his weekly scrubbing with an occasional dip in the local stream, which carried water north to San Francisco Bay.

On Sundays, Jesse conducted a worship service for the family and farm workers. Occasionally neighbors came by to participate. Sarah would pray, Jesse would have a younger person read the scripture, and he would then make his comments on it, inviting others to participate. The service closed with another prayer. A central feature of the prayers was thanks to God for sending the rain in season and for the good crop yields they were experiencing.

The hymns were simple, as there were no hymnals. "Amazing Grace" and "Shall We Gather by the River" were favorites. Occasionally they would sing the "Battle Hymn of the Republic." At first Jim Henry stood in shock at the sound of what he had considered the battle hymn of the Unionists—the enemy that allowed thousands of his fellow prisoners to die at Camp Douglas for lack of proper treatment. For four verses he stood silent. Then as he heard the words "let us live to make men free," he remembered working with Jim at home and the auctioneer selling the family of slaves in Fayetteville. With tears in his eyes, he joined loudly in the singing of the final verse. Still, he could not get over his ill feeling toward Union leaders, including Abraham Lincoln, who as commander-in-chief allowed the conditions that existed at Camp Douglas.

During harvest seasons, Jim Henry, Jesse, and Thad loaded wagons with fruit and grain to take to market in San Jose. They sold to townspeople and wholesalers who would ship it to San Francisco.

While in San Jose, Jim Henry began looking for a wedding ring for Julia. He found gold affordable, but diamonds were beyond his means. After his second crop year, he bought a gold wedding ring which he kept with him at all times, along with the locket containing Julia's photograph. Anytime he was feeling low or lonesome, he would pull them out and think of her and their future.

San Jose's warm sunny days, with just enough rainfall at the right times, seemed to make every year a good crop year, which was just the opposite of what Jim Henry had experienced during his last three years in Yadkin County. He had prospered in 1869 as a sharecropper and as a cash renter in 1870 and 1871. By the end of the 1871 crop season, he had accumulated $4,000 plus farm equipment, two horses, and enough seed for the next crop. He decided it was a good time to sell out and go back and marry Julia.

He sold his horses, farm equipment, and seed to Thad, who was ready to start his own farming operation. It was easy to arrive at the terms, because of their good relationship. They finally settled on a figure of $1,000. Jim Henry left $4,700 in the bank and held $300 cash for the trip back East.

By this time, the Transcontinental Railroad had been completed and he had enough money that working his way back by sea was not even a consideration. He wanted to get back to Julia the fastest way possible.

21

Leaving California

—•◆•—

San Jose's farming conditions and easy access to good markets were so much better than the situation he had known in Yadkin County that he began to think ever more seriously about making a life in California. He could go back to Yadkin County only long enough to marry Julia and say good-bye to their families and friends. He thought of writing Julia about what he was thinking, but then he thought such an issue was too important to discuss other than in person. He did not want to put any issue in the way of their marriage, and he debated with himself as to how hard he should press if Julia objected to moving across the country. He knew their families would not want them to go, but he hoped they would not stand in the way. He wished he had a way to talk with Julia in order to relieve the tension in his own mind as to whether he was going home for good or whether he would be back with her.

In early December 1871, three years from the time he had left, Jim Henry began his return to North Carolina, this time traveling by train across the country.

Jim Henry started his trip in an older coach with uncomfortable wooden seats with backs at ninety degrees. As his trip progressed, he found accommodation in newer cars with padded seats. Some of the express trains even had sleepers, but not at a price he could afford. Dining cars offered ordinary fare at extraordinary prices. He found that most passengers ate food they had carried with them or purchased from vendors during fifteen-minute stops at stations along the way.

During daylight hours, Jim Henry rode next to the window and observed the scenery, which was spectacular during the long uphill climb from Sacramento to Truckee near Lake Tahoe at the top of the Sierra mountain range. Rain fell as the train climbed. He heard the sound of the locomotive change from a slow steady chug to a frenzy of fast chugs as the drive wheels spun wildly without effect. The engineer stopped the engine and started off again with slow chugs, which would gradually become more frequent as the train began to pick up speed.

Once they crossed the top of the Sierras and began to descend toward Reno, Nevada, the air became dry and clear, and it seemed to Jim Henry that he could see forever. It made him feel good that there was one less mountain range between him and Julia.

As they crossed the dry desert wastelands of Nevada and Utah, Jim Henry noted a few feeble attempts at farming in spots where the railroad crossed small stream beds. By comparison, Yadkin County did not seem so bad after all. If farmers could farm out here, Jim Henry thought, they could certainly farm in Yadkin County.

In Omaha, Jim Henry and the other passengers had to cross the Missouri River from Nebraska into Iowa by steam ferry, as the railroad bridge was not scheduled for completion until 1873. Large drays pulled up alongside the train and transported passengers, luggage, and freight to the ferry landing. Jim Henry was impressed with the size and fast current of the Missouri. Due to the current, the steam ferry pilot had to crab strongly upstream in order to go straight across. Other drays picked them up upon landing and transported them to the train station in Council Bluffs, Iowa. There Jim Henry boarded a train bound for Chicago on the Chicago, Burlington & Quincy Railroad.

Jim Henry chose to break up his trip for a day in the small

town of Union, Iowa, where he knew a significant percentage of the population came from Yadkin County. He got off the train, walked to the business section of the small town, and began asking people, "Are you from Yadkin County, North Carolina?"

His inquiries quickly elicited a response from a pretty blonde woman who said, "I cannot claim to be from North Carolina, but I would be more than pleased to show you the sights."

"What sights?" Jim Henry asked.

She jiggled her ample breasts and said, "Just whatever sights you want to see."

Jim Henry saw her invitation as a proposition and said, "No thanks." He turned away and resumed asking people whether they were from Yadkin County.

Soon Jim Henry found a man from Yadkin County. Although they were not kin and did not even know each other's families, the man was interested in helping when Jim Henry told him he would be there for only one night and would like to have a chance to meet local residents who came from North Carolina, particularly Yadkin County. Jim Henry also asked the man for a recommendation of a hotel where he could stay and meet with people. The man said, "The only hotel in town is a bawdyhouse with a saloon downstairs. Nobody you want to see will want to meet with you there. I would suggest the Friends Meeting House. It's right in the middle of town. Our pastor is from North Carolina, and I'll get word to several others from back home."

Jim Henry exclaimed, "That would be perfect. What time?"

"Let's say six o'clock."

Jim Henry was amazed at his good fortune and asked one further favor. "Is there a photographer in town who could make me a picture like this one?" He opened up the small case and showed the man Julia's image. "She gave it to me three years ago when I left North Carolina. I wished that I had one to give her, but I did not have one and couldn't afford one. I am on the way back to her

A print made from a daguerreotype of James (Jim) Henry Shore, who wrote on the back of the print, "Made in Union, Iowa, Nov. 1871, on way home from Cal. Went to Cal. Dec. 15, 1867. Got home from Federal prison June 1865."

and really want to give her my photograph."

The man then took him to the photographer's studio and left him there. Jim Henry posed as the photographer put his head under the black curtain at the back of the camera and set off the flash powder. The man promised to have it developed by closing time that afternoon.

While waiting for the photo to be developed, Jim Henry checked into his hotel room, took a much-needed bath in the bathroom at the end of the hall, and then went back to the photographer's studio. The photograph was still slightly damp from the chemical baths. The photographer recommended that it be left overnight to dry thoroughly. The first thing the next morning, he would mount it under the glass in a frame. Jim Henry thought the photograph did not flatter him, but he knew Julia wouldn't care.

That evening, he went to the church and found that quite a few Yadkin natives had not only come, they had brought food with them. Among the things people brought to eat were ham, boiled eggs, and homemade pies, which reminded him of home. As they enjoyed their meal, they talked of their family members still in North Carolina, mutual friends in Yadkin County, and of their experiences in Iowa. Most had been drawn to Iowa by the availability of good land at bargain prices. They showed Jim Henry an advertisement by the Iowa Railroad Land Company for 1,700,000 acres in Iowa and 180,000 acres in eastern Nebraska "as fertile and desirable as any in America, at $8 to $10 per acre." The only negative note anyone expressed was that with so many people plowing up the prairie grasses to farm, there was less moisture in the ground. Each year, the wind blew up more and more dust.

Jim Henry told those present of his plan to marry Julia Williams. No one knew her, but several people recognized the name of her father, Crawford Wade Williams, who had represented Yadkin County in the North Carolina Senate in the 1850s.

As they said their good-byes, everyone asked Jim Henry to extend greetings to friends and family back home. Jim Henry thanked them for their gracious hospitality and walked back to his hotel. As he passed the downstairs saloon, he glanced about and saw that the girl who had propositioned him was not there. That night he prayed that she found another way to make a living.

The next morning, Jim Henry picked up his photograph and boarded the train for Chicago.

22

The Return Home

*J*im Henry was well aware of the Great Chicago Fire at the time it occurred, not long before he left California. Word of the tragedy traveled throughout the country and captivated people's attention. He looked forward to seeing the destruction firsthand. He wondered whether it signified some form of divine retribution for the wrongs perpetrated in that city against prisoners at Camp Douglas and against citizens who sought to help them.

He stepped off the train in downtown Chicago with two hours to spend before he needed to catch the next train for Philadelphia—just enough time to look over what had been Chicago's downtown. He saw block after block of cleared areas, where buildings large and small had once stood in the central city. Except for a few skeletons of large buildings, the structures were all gone. In their place were piles of debris, which were in the process of being loaded onto trucks and carried away. Large vacant areas testified that much debris had already been carried away. Surveyors were at work, preparing for the widening of streets and the rebuilding of the city on a grander scale than before.

Jim Henry had thought he would feel sorry for the people of Chicago, but as he surveyed the scene, he felt sorry only about the deaths and injuries that occurred, and not about the physical damage. He concluded from the extensive preparations for rebuilding that most of the structures were covered by fire insurance and that most people suffered little except from temporary interruption of their businesses and the need to obtain temporary housing until new houses could be built.

When Jim Henry purchased his ticket for Philadelphia, he looked at the list of waypoint stations and realized he was following the same train track on which he had ridden at government expense after the end of the war. As the train pulled out of Chicago and headed south along the western shore of Lake Michigan, he looked for Camp Douglas, but did not see it. He asked the well-dressed gentleman sitting beside him what had happened to Camp Douglas. The man replied, "It was closed down and dismantled right after the war, and the land has all been developed. Why do you ask?"

"I was a prisoner there once."

"Young man, you are lucky to be alive. They say 6,000 prisoners died there. Nobody will ever know for sure how many. The government destroyed all the records when it closed the camp."

Jim Henry replied, "Thanks for telling me that hell hole no longer exists. The fact that it is gone may help me get it out of my mind."

Jim Henry closed his eyes and pretended to sleep, but could not keep his mind from flashing back to the dying men he had seen along the open sewer behind the latrines and the wagons leaving the camp each morning laden with bodies wrapped in blankets and stacked on top of each other. He prayed that the Lord would take these memories away or at least keep him from dwelling further on them.

In no time at all, his mind shifted from Camp Douglas to Julia. He began to rehearse in his mind how he would go to her house, find her, and sweep her into a long embrace. Then they would determine a very early date for their marriage. Jim Henry thought about how he would bring up the idea of their going to California to live. He had written to let her know he planned to come home in mid-December. The more he thought about Julia, the more excited he became. He brought his feigned nap to an end, reached into his pocket, and pulled out her photo.

As he looked at the photo, he was so excited that he showed it to the man beside him and said, "That's who I am going back home to marry. I haven't seen her in three years."

"Mighty attractive woman," said the man. "Three years is a long time. Are you sure she'll be there waiting for you?"

Jim Henry told the man how their love had survived enough forced separations that he was sure she would be waiting.

"At least this time she knows I am coming back," he said. "Last time most people thought I was dead and that I would not be coming back. She believed in my return even when she couldn't know." Then Jim Henry described the circumstances of their current separation in detail.

A tear glistened in the man's eye as he said, "There can be no doubt. She will be there for you."

Just before the train reached Philadelphia, Jim Henry thought about the wonderful meal he had been given at the Soldiers Home. He asked the man whether it was still there. The man told him, "There used to be two such homes in Philadelphia, but they both closed soon after the war was over."

Jim Henry said, "One of them was near the rail station. That is where I had my first good meal in over a year. Thanks for keeping me from wasting any time looking for it." With that he told the man he had enjoyed traveling with him and ran to the ticket windows to buy his ticket to Washington.

The trip from Philadelphia through Baltimore to Washington was one of anticipation, because he had never been to the nation's capital. The Pennsylvania Railroad's station in Washington was on the edge of the National Mall, which offered Jim Henry a chance to view the Capitol Building and the partially built Washington Monument, whose construction had been halted prior to the Civil War. Now that the war had been over for six years, construction of the monument had been resumed with a slightly different shade of gray stone.

He was glad that in the six years since the war ended, the rail lines between North and South had been rebuilt. Jim Henry was able to travel to Petersburg by rail instead of steamboat as he had done before. Yet he remembered the exhilaration the former prisoners felt as they jumped into the Chesapeake Bay for a swim.

Memories of his return from the war continued to flood his mind as the train took him from Petersburg to Danville and on to Greensboro. How nice it was to be riding in a coach rather than on top of a boxcar at night in the rain. But when he reached Greensboro, the distinction between the two trips began to fade. There still was no rail service from Greensboro to Salem, where the community feared that a railroad would bring noise, smoke, risk of fires, and undesirable strangers into the area.

This time, however, he was able to hitch a few wagon rides from people going his way. He was so excited about coming home to Julia that he told the wagon drivers about where he had been and how he was coming home after three years, having made enough money for them to get married and start farming. One driver had been drinking and must have figured Jim Henry was coming home with a lot of money. Jim Henry watched the man's demeanor and was worried that he had been talking too much. Suddenly the man reached back into the wagon for a rifle. Before he could get to it, Jim Henry tried to throw him off the wagon. The man attempted to reach back for the gun, but Jim Henry grabbed it first. The man said, "I wasn't going to do anything."

Jim Henry replied, "I am sure you weren't, but just to make sure, let me hold the weapon while we ride."

The man drove nervously until they reached a point where his and Jim Henry's routes diverged. Then Jim Henry fired the single shot muzzle loader to make sure it could not quickly be fired again, thanked the man for the ride, and hurried out of gun range. From then on until he reached home, Jim Henry refrained from telling strangers the details of where he had been and why he was coming back.

That night he stayed at the Salem Tavern, which had fallen on hard times during the Reconstruction period but was still in operation. Jim Henry found a new owner in charge. Mr. Butner had bought the operation from the Moravian Church, as business was down and the church needed money to build the Salem College campus.

Jim Henry had hoped to find a guest with whom he could find a ride to Yadkin County, but there were very few guests and none heading for Yadkin. The moment the dining room opened early the next morning, he ordered ham and eggs with grits for breakfast and fried chicken, bread, and apples to take on his remaining twenty-eight-mile journey. He topped off the water in his canteen, threw his knapsack across his shoulders, and set out on foot for Glenn's Ferry.

At midday, he reached the Yadkin River. As he was the sole passenger, the ferryman asked if he would mind waiting a bit to see if other passengers might come along. Jim Henry said, "Ordinarily I would not mind waiting, but I have been gone for three years and the most beautiful girl in the world has been waiting for me all that time in Boonville. I need to get there right away." With that the ferryman cast off the mooring line and adjusted the lines that held the pulleys that ran along the cable stretched across the Yadkin.

Jim Henry ate his small dinner as he rode on the ferry to save time. He bid farewell to the ferryman, who wished him a happy return to his woman. He then hiked from the river across the bottomlands, past the Glenwood mansion and on to his grandparents' home three miles north and near the river. His grandfather, John Shore, had died in 1867, but his grandmother, Susanna Arney Shore, still lived in the house with her son Calvin and his family. When Susanna Shore saw Jim Henry, she shed tears of joy, just as she had when he returned from the war six years earlier. Again, Jim Henry's Uncle Calvin offered to drive Jim Henry home in a wagon, but Jim Henry knew it would be dark before his uncle Calvin could return home. More importantly, a wagon was just too slow.

Jim Henry said, "That is a mighty kind offer, but I wonder if you could just lend me a horse for a day or so until I can bring it back to you."

Uncle Calvin helped Jim Henry saddle a fresh horse, and in less than two hours Jim Henry had ridden the fourteen miles home. As he pulled up in front of the old log house, his mother, Eunice, came running out crying, "Praise the Lord!" They embraced for only a moment before she broke away to shout, "Jack! Boys! Jim Henry's here! Come on in!"

"Let me show you how to call 'em." Jim Henry pulled a large conch shell from his bag and blew it like a trumpet. The roar from the heavy shell echoed through the quiet countryside, and almost immediately Jack and the five boys began emerging from barn and field. Jim Henry was thrilled to be surrounded by his family members, who were overjoyed at his return.

Jim Henry was amazed at how much his brothers had matured during the three years he was away. Quill was now twenty years old, Bill was twenty, John Wesley eighteen, Sanders ten, and Wiley eight. The older three were now taller than he, and the two younger ones seemed big enough for farm work. It was good to see his family had a good labor supply without him.

The younger boys wanted to blow the conch shell, and Jim Henry showed them how and told them how he had obtained it in Panama. Then he cut their happy reunion short and asked if he could go wash up and use one of the horses to go see someone special.

Again, Jim Henry set out at a fast trot and then a gallop for the last two miles of his day's journey of thirty miles on foot and by horse, which came on top of a journey of similar length the day before. Yet he did not feel tired. His heart was racing, not from exertion, but from anticipation of seeing Julia. He allowed the horse to settle into a trot for a little while, but his eagerness to see Julia soon caused him to prod the horse back into a gallop the rest of the way.

The Wade Williams family's large home was situated behind a white picket fence near the crossroads that marked the center of Boonville.

Suddenly, he became aware of loud sounds of cheers and clapping coming from Julia's family members, who had assembled on the front porch. He had hoped for an opportunity to talk at length with Julia and to resolve the matter of moving to California with her before discussing it with their families. It appeared he could not gracefully avoid an immediate extended visit with her family. He feared they would ask about his plans for the future.

Jim Henry was quickly surrounded by members of Julia's family, but Julia herself was nowhere to be seen. He was overwhelmed by the Williamses' welcome, but wanted only to know where his Julia was. He had a moment to peer through the front window as he saw Julia cleaning the table before their supper. At that moment, her attention was grabbed by the commotion on the porch and she looked up, through the same window. When their eyes met, her face paled with surprise and complete euphoria. She dropped the dinner plate and made her way to the front door. As she moved through the threshold, Wade Williams chuckled and announced to the family on the porch, "I know we all have missed Jim Henry, but not as much as Julia has. Let us leave them to a moment alone. Come on inside so we can finish setting up for supper."

Julia and Jim Henry were both bursting with excitement and joy as they hugged and kissed for what seemed to be an eternity to them and those secretly watching. Someone inside started clapping and the entire company joined in thunderous applause with shouts of blessing and congratulations. As the crowd squeezed into the home for supper, the pastor of the Williamses' local Methodist Church gave praise and thanks to the Lord for bringing Julia and Jim Henry back together in love.

During the bustle of dinner preparations, Jim Henry whispered to Julia, "I surely would like to take you with me to California to live."

"Are you serious?"

"It would offer a lot of opportunity."

"I know the Bible says 'whither thou goest, I will go,' and you know I will, but we need to make sure we are making the right choice about where to spend our lives."

"We certainly do not need to decide right now, but I wanted to mention the idea to you before we are asked about our plans."

"As long as it is just an idea, you can mention it to anyone." Then she added, "Some may not think much of it."

The Williams family was excited to share a meal with Jim Henry and peppered him with questions about his experiences over the past three years. He was moved by the warmth of his reception by the family until Wade Williams asked him, "Have you had a chance to make any plans as to what you will be doing now that you are back?"

"I plan to farm." Then he added, "I found the conditions were quite good in California for successful farming." He went on to explain the favorable growing conditions, the ease of transporting crops to market, and the strong market prices."

"Are you considering doing your farming out there?" Wade asked.

When Jim Henry replied, "It certainly is something to consider," the warm reception he had enjoyed became quite chilly.

Wade exclaimed, "Do you really mean you would leave family and friends here to go out there to stay?"

Jim Henry did not want to let on that he had not mentioned the idea to his parents and simply said, "We would come back from time to time on the train. It doesn't take but a week or so, and one day the railroad will come a lot closer to Boonville than Greensboro. Certainly it will come as far as Salem and there is talk of it coming all the way to Crutchfield, just two miles from Boonville." Jim Henry's best arguments seemed to fall on deaf ears, and he was pleased when Julia spoke up.

"Daddy, Jim Henry just got here. Let's not talk about anything except how glad we are to see him. I want to hear about what he has seen over the past three years."

He recounted the highlights of his travels to New York, Panama, California, and back. He managed to include a full description of the profitability of farming in San Jose.

After supper, Jim Henry invited Julia to take a walk, and they got their coats and went outside. As soon as they got to the porch, he said, "We need to talk about California." For the next three hours they huddled in each other's arms on the porch as Jim Henry recounted his experiences in California, his love and respect for the Jesse Hobson family, the profitability of farming in San Jose, and the growing conditions and economic factors that made it so.

Finally, he asked Julia if she would try to persuade her father to withdraw his objection to the idea of their going to California. She agreed to try to speak to her father alone about it in the morning, and Jim Henry promised to come back after dinner the next afternoon. Jim Henry rode home in pale moonlight. The mid-December moon was in its first quarter, and the half disk reflected just enough light to see the road. He took comfort in the knowledge that the horse's night vision was better than his own. Since they could safely travel only at a walk, it was well after midnight when they reached the Shore home.

He found a lighted lantern in front of the house and used it to stable the horse and find his way into the cabin, where he found a rope bed nicely made up for him. As he drifted off to sleep, he prayed that Julia would have success with her father.

———◆———

The next morning the family woke up well before sunrise and started on their pre-breakfast chores. Jim Henry roused himself, ready to help, ready to be part of the family again, but Jack and Eunice insisted that he should try to sleep until breakfast. He couldn't go back to sleep because he kept thinking how he would explain his desire to go to California.

Once the chores were done and the family gathered for breakfast, he told them the highlights of his travels and especially about his business success in San Jose and the friendship of the Hobson family.

"Julia and I will be getting married soon, and I believe we have a better chance of prospering there than we'll have here. I've asked her to think about moving to California."

No one spoke for a moment. Then Eunice said, "It has been bad enough having you out there for three years. I can't bear to lose you for good." Her voice cracked, and Jack cleared his throat as if a lump the size of an egg had formed in it.

Jim Henry could tell that no one else in the family wanted to pursue that avenue of conversation, and he dropped it.

That afternoon, Jim Henry met Julia on the Williamses' porch, and from her countenance he could tell that the conversation between her and her father had not gone well.

"I tried to persuade him," she said, "but after telling him all the advantages of being in San Jose, I am satisfied he will never give his blessing or even his consent to our marriage if it means we move to California. He thinks it is a choice between family and money."

"He is right that family is more important than money. Mom is not too keen on the idea, either. I was just hoping we could go out there and still maintain family ties. I will just have to get the idea of going out to California out of my mind. After all, marrying you is what is really on my mind."

Jim Henry took the photograph Julia had given him of herself out of his pocket, opened the cover, and said, "I looked at your picture every day for three years. Here's one for you." Then he gave her the photograph he had made in Uniontown, Iowa. Before she could finish saying, "I love it," he reached into his pocket again and produced the gold ring he had brought from California. He got down on one knee and asked, "Will you marry me?"

"Yes, yes, yes."

They held each other in a tight embrace and he finally said, "It is time for me to speak with your father."

Jim Henry knocked on the door and heard Wade Williams invite him in. As he entered, he saw that Mr. Williams was alone in the parlor.

"Mr. Williams, may I have a word with you?"

Mr. Williams stood and greeted Jim Henry somewhat stiffly and invited him to sit down.

Jim Henry got right to the point. "Mr. Williams, Julia tells me you cannot reconcile yourself to the idea of our going to California."

"She told you right. Her mother and I would never get over it. It would be almost like a death in the family. California is too far. You should have seen Julia moping around here these past three years. We might be moping around here the same way for the rest of our lives. Besides, there are things I can do to help you get started in farming here that I cannot do if you are on the other side of the country."

"Mr. Williams, I have loved Julia practically all my life and now I want to marry her and love her all the rest of our lives together. We want your blessing, and we want you to know we plan to stay right here and not move to California."

Before Jim Henry could say another word, Wade jumped to his feet and cut him off. "It's about time you two got married! If you've given up the California foolishness, you have my permission and my blessing. May you find all the joy her mother and I have found in marriage."

One month later, on January 23, 1872, Julia and Jim Henry were married in the Boonville Methodist Church. Wedding attendants included Jim Henry's five brothers and Julia's two surviving sisters, Martha and Permelia, and her two surviving brothers, Jim and John.

Jim Henry and Julia were both attached to the farm near Boonville where Julia had grown up, before the Williamses were made to move away. When Jim Henry asked Wade if he'd consider selling it, he found that his father-in-law was willing, and made the young couple a good price.

"We will live in the old cabin until we can build a new home on the property your father is selling us," Jim Henry told Julia. "Then I will build you a fine house for our family, God willing."

AFTERWORD

T he deed of sale that made the farm Jim Henry and Julia's was recorded in 1874. The young couple stayed close to family, but they also established their own ways. Rather than attend the Booneville Methodist church which the Williams family attended, or the Deep Creek Quaker Church with the Shores, they joined the Boonville Baptist Church that met in the church building adjacent to Jim Henry Shore's and Julia Williams's childhood homes and where they first attended school. That was where they first fell in love, after all.

Jim Henry Shore's family farm.

Portrait of Jim Henry Shore and Julia Williams Shore in middle age.

Jim Henry Shore on his horse "Bill" circa 1920.

Family photo at Jim Henry Shore's home.

Jim Henry Shore and wife Julia Ann Williams Shore in a photo taken about 1910.

Jim Henry and Julia's immediate family at their home. Seated are Jim Henry and Julia Williams Shore. Standing are Martha Augusta Shore Garland (Mattie), Dr. Thaddeus Warsaw Shore (known as Thad or Dr. T.W.), John Wade Shore, and Annie Pearl Shore Davis.

Jim Henry and Julia expanded the farm to 600 acres. Later, they bought another 400 acres of farmland along the Yadkin River. He drove his buggy back and forth to supervise both operations until he was well into his eighties. For many years he brought more tobacco to the warehouse in Winston-Salem than any other single farmer in Yadkin County.

He was a symbol of hope to members of the community who at the time of his death were struggling through the Great Depression, for they knew that he had seen far worse and yet went on to live a good life.

Photo of a Civil War reunion held in 1915. Jim Henry Shore is seated with his cane on the far right.

Among those at the funeral were son Thaddeus ("Thad"), the local country doctor and nationally known field trial competitor and judge; the author's grandmother Annie Pearl, a teacher, hospital volunteer, and wife of businessman and civic leader Egbert Lawrence Davis, Sr.; and John Wade Shore, Sr. ("Wade"), an outstanding baseball player at North Carolina State University, a school teacher, mayor of Boonville, and founder and president of the Commercial and Savings Bank, Boonville, North Carolina.

Jim Henry Shore dressed for work on his farm.

Jim Henry Shore's story shows how love and faith can enable a person to be undaunted by the worst privations and go on to have a good life. His story also shows a spiritual quality that suggests he was not only a man's man and a woman's man, but also God's man.

BIBLIOGRAPHY

Brewer, Paul. The Civil War State by State. San Diego: Thunder Bay Press. 2004.

Brumfield, Lewis. Historical Architecture of Yadkin County, North Carolina. Yadkinville: Yadkin County Historical Society. 1987.

Bunn, Maude. The Genealogy of Marion-Davis Families. Raleigh: Edwards and Broughton Company. 1973.

Catton, Bruce. American Heritage Picture History of the Civil War. New York: Gramercy. 1994.

Casstevens, Frances H. Clingman's Brigade in the Confederacy, 1862–1865. Jefferson and London: McFarland and Company. 2009.

Davis, Burke. The Civil War: Strange and Fascinating Facts. New York: Wings Books. 1994.

Denney, Robert E. Civil War Prisons and Escapes: A Day-By-Day Chronicle. New York: Sterling Publishing Company. 1993.

Eicher, John H., and David J. Eicher. Civil War High Commands. Stanford: Stanford University Press, 2001.

Foner, Eric. Reconstruction: America's Unfinished Revolution, 1863–1877. New York: Perennial. 2002.

Hughes, Nathaniel. Sir Henry Morton Stanley, Confederate. Baton Rouge: Louisiana State University Press. 2000.

Hoots, Carl. Cemeteries of Yadkin County, North Carolina. Spartanburg: The Reprint Company. 1985.

Johnson, Curt, and Mark McLaughlin. Civil War Battles. New York: Fairfax Press. 1977.

Lee, Henry. A Civil War Diary. Black Mountain: Craggy Mountain Press. 1997.

Levy, George. To Die in Chicago: Confederate Prisoners at Camp Douglas 1862–65. Gretna, La.: Pelican Publishing Company. 1999.

Martin, Iain C.. The Quotable American Civil War. Guilford, Conn.: Lyons Press. 2008.

Meier, Heinz. Memoirs of a Swiss Officer in the American Civil War. Bern: Herbert Land and Co. 1972.

Nathan, Adele. The Building of the First Transcontinental Railroad. New York: Random House. 1950.

Shore, Leoria. Ancestors and Descendants of Frederick Shore. Hillsboro: Multi Business Press. 1983.

Shore, Leoria. The Frederick Shore Family: 1570–1980 from Switzerland to North Carolina. Hillsboro: Multi Business Press. 1983.

Shore family records compiled by the late Marvin Shore and left in the safekeeping of the Moravian Archives of Winston-Salem, North Carolina.

ACKNOWLEDGMENTS

The author is indebted to his father, Egbert Lawrence Davis, Jr. (1911–2006), who, when asked what he most liked about his "Grandpa Shore," replied, "Because he would talk to me." He knew the story of James Henry Shore and his wife Julia Williams Shore was worth telling, especially the true story of their fulfilled promises to wait years for each other.

Lewis Brumfield of Yadkinville was generous in making available his time and extensive historical knowledge as we explored the history of the Shore and Williams families and the Yadkin County setting of this narrative.

The late Henry Fleming Shore of Boonville shared childhood recollections of and family stories about his grandfather. Henry's late sister, Elizabeth ("Lib") Shore Reece of Boonville, also shared childhood memories of her grandfather. The author's cousin, Elizabeth ("Betsy") Smith Waud of Mill Valley, California, solved the mystery as to why there seemed to be no official tax or census record of James Henry Shore's presence in California during the period of 1868–1871. Using internet resources and her skills as a professional genealogist, she searched the records for Californians who were listed as having James Henry Shore's date and place of birth. She found that the name "James Henry Share," which was listed in California tax and census records for 1869–1871, was actually a misspelling of James Henry Shore's name. That finding led to the discovery from tax records where and with whom he lived while in California. It resulted in documenting his presence in various Union prison facilities through which he passed during his confinement as a prisoner of war. It also led to the identification of some of his records in the North Carolina Office of Archives and History. Apparently, Union authorities misspelled his name when he was captured and kept on using the wrong name on the official form each time he was processed into a new facility—even on the form that cited that he had taken an oath of allegiance to the United States at the time of his release. There can be no doubt that he used this document as proof of his citizenship when he sailed to California.

The author is also indebted to James Henry Smith, named for James Henry Shore, and his brother, Bobby Lee Smith, whose families now own and cultivate what was once James Henry Shore's land.

The author wishes to express appreciation for the hospitality of the present owners of Tyre Glen's Glenwood mansion and the kind assistance of the staff members of the North Carolina Office of Archives and History; the Morganton Public Library, Morganton, North Carolina; and the Museum of the Middle Appalachians, Saltville, Virginia.

The author also wishes to thank his sister Anne Davis Hummel for collecting high-resolution photographs included in this book.

The author acknowledges the outstanding editorial work on this book by Nora Gaskin Esthimer, Kelly Prelipp Lojk, Douglas Hipps, Linda and Liliana Yager, the author's son Egbert ("Bert") Lawrence Davis IV, and the author's beloved wife, Sandra Holderness Davis.

Finally, the author appreciates the encouragement and helpful comments of leaders and participants in workshops of the North Carolina Writers Network.

ABOUT THE AUTHOR

Lawrence Davis is a native of Winston-Salem, North Carolina. He is a graduate of Princeton University (Woodrow Wilson School of Public and International Affairs-History, Economics, and Politics 1960), Duke Law School (1963), and George Washington University (M.B.A.1966). He served two years in the U.S. Army Intelligence Corps, attaining the rank of captain. He then joined the Womble law firm serving in Winston-Salem and Raleigh for more than fifty years, during which time he served two terms in the N.C. House and the N.C. Senate. He was inducted into the Order of the Long Leaf Pine.

Lawrence grew up with stories of his ancestors' lives and is pleased to bring them to life in his first published novel. He lives in Raleigh, North Carolina, with his wife, Sandra Holderness Davis. Their children, Alexandra Hipps, Bert Davis, Lucinda Davis, and Pam Davis, all live in North Carolina.

Made in USA - Kendallville, IN
1125403_9781733681650
06 19 2020 0809